**'You want me to **

Louise tried to clari[..]
the most rational m[..]

'Certainly not! That [..] at all!'
Jacob's leanly elega[..] hands had clenched
into powerful-looking fists and his accent was
growing stronger by the minute. 'You will be
Aletta's mother. You understand? We must
be married.'

'Married!' Louise felt all the breath leave her
lungs in a rush as if she had been punched.

**Dear Reader**

We look at special care baby units with Josie Metcalfe's SECRETS TO KEEP, Caroline Anderson returns to the obstetrics unit—more babies—at the Audley Memorial in ANYONE CAN DREAM, while each heroine has a secret to keep from the hero. You will *love* William and Jacob! We welcome back Sharon Wirdnam with CASUALTY OF PASSION, Meredith Webber's UNRULY HEART repatriates ill people, and both books bring couples back together. A good month's reading!

*The Editor*

**Josie Metcalfe** lives in Cornwall now with her long-suffering husband, four children and two horses, but as an Army brat frequently on the move, books became the only friends who came with her wherever she went. Now that she writes them herself she is making new friends and hates saying goodbye at the end of a book—but there are always more characters in her head clamouring for attention until she can't wait to tell their stories.

Recent titles by the same author:

NO ALTERNATIVE

# SECRETS
# TO KEEP

BY
JOSIE METCALFE

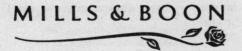

# MILLS & BOON

# MILLS & BOON LIMITED
ETON HOUSE, 18-24 PARADISE ROAD
RICHMOND, SURREY TW9 1SR

*MILLS & BOON, the Rose Device and LOVE ON CALL
are trademarks of the publisher.*

*First published in Great Britain 1994
by Mills & Boon Limited*

© Josie Metcalfe 1994

*Australian copyright 1994   Philippine copyright 1995
This edition 1995*

ISBN 0 263 78970 5

*Set in Times 10 on 11½ pt. by
Rowland Phototypesetting Limited
Bury St Edmunds, Suffolk*

03-9502-47608

*Made and printed in Great Britain*

# CHAPTER ONE

THE tall man stood quietly in the shadows, watching. From the glassed-in area of Sister's office the whole of the ward was visible, but his gaze was fixed on one of the occupants.

The rustle of a starched apron caught his ear as Sister Wilson entered.

'Oh! Mr den Haag! I'm sorry, I didn't know you were here. Can I help you at all?' She was a little flustered to find him in her office. It was partly the unannounced presence of the eminent paediatrician but also because he was a very attractive man.

He was tall, several inches over six feet, with the broad, powerful-looking shoulders that would not seem inappropriate on a manual labourer or an athlete at the peak of his career.

But for all the impression of power imparted by his build there was a quality of stillness about him, a quiet watchfulness which subconsciously reassured smaller, weaker beings that all that potential force was held well under control.

He shook his head as he moved from the shadowy corner into the pool of light cast by the lamp on her desk, his steps silent and smooth as the light caught on the silver-gilt strands of hair brushed neatly back from his elegant brow.

'I needed to check on baby Roberts.' His voice was deep and soft, pitched quietly to suit the time of night and his surroundings as he gestured with one long, lean-fingered hand towards the other tiny pool of light.

'And Sister Harris up on Obstetrics caught me on my way. She's concerned about Mrs Roberts. How do you think she's coping with the situation? It doesn't look as if she's going to get any sleep without a sedative.'

He glanced once more towards the diminutive figure in the ward full of babies. From this distance she seemed to be no more than a child herself. Her slight figure and halo of curly amber-coloured hair made her look like a dainty Christmas angel as she sat beside the incubator watching the tiny figure of the child she had given birth to with such anguish that morning.

She was perched on the edge of the seat, her whole being concentrated on the child as if she was willing him to survive with her whole strength.

'Mr den Haag? We were so sorry to hear about your wife, sir.' Sister Wilson's voice startled him as she broke in on his thoughts, and she misread his reaction. 'I'm sorry, sir. The hospital grapevine, you know. I don't think there's a single member of the staff who hasn't heard. How is she? The coma's not irreversible, is it?'

His large frame was totally still for a moment before he visibly forced himself into movement and shook his head.

'You've probably heard she's in Intensive Care on life-support?' She nodded her agreement.

'There are no cranial reflexes and a flat EEG at maximum gain,' his voice sounded hollow. 'Evans-Jones and Tomlinson will be repeating the tests in the morning. The tests would have been done again after six hours for the possibility of organ donation, but. . . but it depends on their findings tomorrow what happens about the baby. . .'

The tone of his voice had changed almost impercepti-bly. His professional manner had been totally evident while he spoke of his wife's desperate medical condition, but when he'd mentioned their unborn child. . .

Jenny Wilson's heart went out to the gentle giant of a man now perched tensely on the papers on the corner of her desk. His lean hands were clenched into fists and the muscles at the corners of his cleanly sculptured jaw bunched rhythmically as he clenched his teeth. Darkly lashed lids closed over stunning sapphire-blue eyes as he drew a deep breath and released it before continuing.

'At present, it looks as if the child is fine, but it is still considerably premature, so the longer. . .' When his voice grew thick in his throat he paused until the professional tone took over once more. 'Well, you know the situation well enough. If the mother can be kept "alive", every day gives the child a better chance of survival.'

The mental torture he had been suffering all day had etched lines of strain on his face and dark shadows had appeared under his eyes, leaving them looking bruised. 'And after the trauma of Mrs Roberts' delivery this morning. . .' He shook his head wearily.

Sister Wilson's gaze flicked towards the diminutive figure almost lost in the gloom. 'Poor woman! How she's coping after everything that's happened to her today, I don't know. I suppose she's clinging to the baby because he's all she's got left now. But even then, he isn't likely to. . .'

Something in her words had caught his attention, and his interest in the conversation sharpened suddenly.

'You are still talking about "our" Mrs Roberts, aren't you? The Special Care Baby Unit special nurse who delivered the spina bifida baby in the early hours of the morning?' His gaze, too, went to the ghostly figure in the other room.

'That's right. It was later on in the morning that her husband finally arrived to visit her. Staff Nurse Yuen let him come in to see the baby even though it wasn't visiting hours, and there was a terrible scene. Matron had to come up, and he was demanding to see you, but you had just gone off-duty and she wouldn't call you back, so he demanded to see the hospital administrator.

'He kept on and on until we took him into that little room we keep for parents to crash out in when there's a crisis.'

He nodded, indicating that he understood her narrative so far, and a thick strand of his silver-blond hair fell forward towards his startlingly dark brows and was swiftly raked back by one lean hand to restore his habitually immaculate appearance.

'He insisted there must have been some mix-up in the name-tags on the child, as the one with his name on could not be his, especially as it was "defective". Then, when Matron insisted that there had not been a mistake as his child had been the only one born this morning, he demanded that his wife should be brought out from the ward!' Her voice was scandalised as she continued.

'Well! You know what a rough time she had with the delivery, with the baby lying so awkwardly and her being so tiny.'

A grimace crossed his face at the memory of the fight they'd had to deliver the child.

Sister Wilson was continuing her narrative.

'But he said if she wasn't brought out of the ward to speak to him then he was going on to the ward!

'Anyway, when she was brought through in a wheelchair, she insisted that everybody else should leave the room, and that she would speak to her husband alone.'

'What did Matron say about that?' His voice was calm, but the tension showed in the clenched fist resting on one taut thigh.

'Matron said only five minutes, as Mrs Roberts wasn't really ready for all that stress, and then they were left together.'

'Well?' he urged her to continue.

'Less than two minutes later he stormed out of the room shouting that he would be seeing his lawyer as soon as he got to his office and start proceedings for a divorce, and he would make damned certain that that "defective monstrosity" never saw a penny of his money!'

'Good God! Why? Did she say what had gone on in there?'

'Not a word. She's always been rather quiet, and since she left the hospital to wait for her baby to be born we lost all contact.'

'That's a shame. She's a damn good nurse.' His eyes were once more fixed on the diminutive figure in the pool of light.

'That's not the end of it,' she warned.

'Lord! What else?'

'Well, we had only just got her back into bed and she had been given a sedative when two policemen arrived on the ward to inform her that her husband had been in an accident just outside the hospital gates and had been killed outright.'

Her final words had left him stunned.

'What!' he was almost speechless. 'Outside the hospital? This morning?' He had been pale with fatigue before, but her last words had totally robbed him of any remaining colour.

Suddenly the significance of what she had said struck Jenny Wilson.

'Oh, my God!' She, too, was lost for words as the implications sank in. 'He was the one who hit your wife's car as she was turning in to the hospital this morning.'

Before she had even opened her eyes, the antiseptic smell told Louise where she was. Slowly, as full consciousness returned, she recognised her surroundings and realised that she was in one of the side rooms off the main hospital ward.

In here, the intrusive bustle of a busy day was muted, leaving a quiet haven in which she could think her private thoughts.

'Oh!' Her hand flew to her stomach. 'Oh, no! It wasn't just a nightmare!' Her voice was husky and her speech slurred with the residue of sedative in her system.

Just one day.

In just one day her whole life had changed. Just a few short hours ago she'd had a husband and a home and the all-too-obvious evidence of the start of their family.

Now. . .?

Her expression was bleak as she contemplated the ruins of the marriage she had entered into with such high hopes.

After her own fatherless childhood, she had so longed to belong to a 'real' family, with a mother and a father who loved each other and their children. She had hoped, too, that when she had married Colin Roberts his parents would have shown her some of the excess of love which they showered on their only son and which she had never known.

Although her mother was alive, Louise didn't live with her, but had been brought up by grandparents who seemed unwilling or perhaps were unable to show their love. Many times during her bleak childhood she had wondered why no one seemed able to love her when she had had so much love to give. So, when she and Colin were married, Louise had hoped that finally she would be allowed inside a charmed family circle.

She had been disillusioned fairly early on in their marriage.

At first she had blamed her lack of satisfaction with Colin's lovemaking on her own starry-eyed expectations, but had slowly started to realise that he was not a gentle man and didn't have the patience to see that she was too inexperienced to cope with his demands.

Still, she consoled herself, it was early days yet and while she would have to accept him as he was for the moment, they loved each other and would eventually sort everything out between them.

Then, exactly one month to the day after their wedding-day, Harold and Betty Roberts had invited themselves to a meal at the lavishly decorated house they had bought for their son and his wife.

'Well, lad?' Harold Roberts had boomed as soon as coats had been removed and sherry glasses distributed. 'Is she pregnant yet?'

Betty Roberts had tut-tutted coyly at her husband's crass bluntness, but Louise had gasped in shock and dropped a full glass of sherry to smash on to the highly polished wood-block floor.

'Louise!' Colin was incensed. 'That glass was one of the Waterford set the Danbys gave us as a wedding present. Now I'll have to buy another set or they'll wonder why we aren't using them when they come to dinner next weekend.'

'Colin, love!' his mother soothed as she crouched swiftly to pick up the larger pieces of crystal. 'Don't you worry about a thing. We'll replace them in time for the Danbys, won't we, Harold?' She glanced up at her husband who stood with his back towards the crackling fire, completely unmoved by the uproar he had caused.

'If you'll excuse me.' Louise's voice was calm—how, she didn't know, but as far as she could tell there was no trace of the searing anger which filled her. 'I'll just check up on the meat.' And with her head held stiffly erect she left the room.

She caught sight of herself in the hugely ornate mirror in the over-decorated hallway and saw large dark eyes gazing almost vacantly back at her, her slightly olive-toned cheeks far paler than usual against the riot of short honey-gold curls.

The smell of the expensive perfume she had dabbed on her pulse points to bolster her confidence seemed far too heavy now, and had started a dull throb behind her eyes.

She hadn't realised that her mother-in-law had followed her until she began to speak.

'Of course, dear, you must have realised that my Colin would do anything to set his Dad's mind at rest. Oh! they're so alike, those two. Do anything for each other, especially my Colin. Always been that way, right from a little boy. And my Harold. Nothing too good for his boy.

'Then,' she continued to chatter as she pushed Louise aside slightly to check her own appearance in the mirror before giving an approving pat to her well-lacquered coiffure, 'when Harold had that funny spell and the doctor warned him to slow down, he told Colin it was about time he did his bit for the next generation

of Robertses and settled down with a nice girl. Someone suitable, you know?'

She hardly paused to take a breath, never mind take
note of how her monologue was being received.

'Well, he's always been a bit of a lad for the girls.
Almost has to beat them off with a stick. Well, you
must have seen the way women chase after him, even
when he was visiting his dad in hospital. . .'

Briefly, Louise's attention wandered.

She had been doing her final stint in ICU, before
she'd decided to specialise in SCBU, when Harold
Roberts had suffered his heart attack and she had been
detailed to 'special' him.

Meeting his son Colin had been inevitable and,
far from being the pursuer, Louise had been the
object of a very determined pursuit herself—not
that Colin had had any intention at the time of offering her marriage! Oh, no! That had been his father's
idea. . .

The voice floated back into focus again. '. . .So he
told his Dad it wouldn't take long before he had his
first grandchild, and probably a few spares for good
measure, just to give you plenty to do while you stay
at home. There'll be time enough for you to start on the
charity committees when they go away to school. . .'

The voice faded out as the full realisation of her
future status hit Louise, and she realised how wilfully
blind her love had made her.

In less than six months Colin's passionate pursuit
had swept her off her feet and up the aisle in a fairy-tale
white gown, filled with an unshakeable belief that she
and Colin had fallen deeply in love with each other.

Now, she saw all too clearly that, once Harold
Roberts had discovered her relationship with the well-
connected Creightons, he had started encouraging

Colin's pursuit. Not because he saw that her fascination with his son's easy charm could grow into a love which could sustain a long and happy marriage, but purely so that she would satisfy his dynastic pretensions.

Never mind that she had worked long and hard to gain her qualifications, and that her position in the Special Care Baby Unit at St Augustine's was a demanding one which she had gained on merit alone. All this was as nothing when they had detected a drop of blue blood!

The rest of the evening passed in a blur, only coming briefly into focus when Harold Roberts paused on the doorstep to dig his son in the ribs with the exhortation to, 'Keep up the good work!'

Sickened by the evening's revelations, Louise resorted to lying to her over-eager spouse to avoid another night of his less than tender attentions.

Colin's disappointed lust made him spiteful, and as he turned his back on her he muttered, 'How am I supposed to enjoy getting you pregnant if you're only one step up from frigid? I'll just have to hope you're as fertile as your mother so I don't have to go through this with you too often!' And he grunted his dissatisfaction as he settled himself to go to sleep.

Would the shocks never end? After the casually cruel revelations his mother had imparted so complacently that evening—and all in a tone which implied that young Louise Creighton should think herself lucky that darling Colin had chosen her as his brood mare—now Colin himself had muttered a half-coherent throwaway line which hinted at a great deal of knowledge about Louise's mother which Louise herself did not know, and which could only have come from her grandparents.

The following day she completed the entry in the

diary she had treated as a confidant since her childhood.

Why should my grandparents have spoken about such private family details to the Roberts?

Just the next day a number of questions were answered.

Louise had written—as usual, care of the family lawyers—to inform her mother that she was getting married.

Although she had hoped that this time would be different, she had not been surprised when her mother did not come to the wedding. After all, when had she ever shown much interest in her daughter?

Now, exactly one month and a day after the event, she had received a letter and, for the first time ever, it contained a return address.

Curiosity vied with fury, and eventually the desire to find the answers to all the questions her grandparents had denied her was stronger than the bitterness her mother's desertion had caused.

When she finally tore open the letter the most important thing she discovered was that her grandparents' lawyer had been instructed to intercept any attempt at regular communication between mother and daughter, including delaying the wedding invitation until it was impossible for her mother to attend. . .

Before Louise had had the opportunity to arrange a confrontation with her grandparents, she had had confirmation that she was pregnant. Unfortunately, the news had coincided with a second long letter from her mother detailing, at Louise's insistence, the true circumstances of the birth of her daughter.

Far from confirming her grandparents' story that

her father had died before Louise had been born, her
mother had enclosed a photograph and the information
that he was very much alive and was now a well
respected doctor in Canada.

Louise had hidden the letter and photograph with
her diary. They were evidence of an unexploded time-
bomb, and she hoped with all her heart that she would
never need to show them to Colin.

Only time would tell.

For several days, while she settled in to her first post
of responsibility in SCBU, Louise searched her heart.
Finally, her priorities became clear.

'It's my baby that matters,' she wrote in her diary
before she chose her next day off to prepare the
traditional special meal to announce the news.

'That's what they all wanted and that's what they're
getting!' she muttered as she viciously stuffed a handful
of blooms into a vase before she realised what she
was doing.

'At least there'll be one person in the world who
loves me just because I'm me.' She ran one hand gently
over her flat stomach. 'And I'll love you, with every
breath in my body,' she vowed emotionally.

In the dark recesses of her mind lurked the fear that
the marriage she had entered into with such high hopes
had little chance of surviving unless she and Colin were
both determined to work at it. She knew that a baby
should never be brought into the world as glue to hold
a marriage together but hoped that, in this case. . .

'Colin is the father of my baby,' she said aloud in the
silence of the gleaming kitchen, 'and I'll do everything I
can to be a good wife and mother.' She heard for
herself the wobble in her voice. 'But no matter what
happens, I'll never desert you.' She stroked her hand

over her stomach in a fervent vow. 'We'll have each other to rely on.'

Bolstered by her decision, she announced her pregnancy, to the coarse delight of her father-in-law and the relief of her husband, who almost immediately vacated her bed on the pretext that he didn't want to do anything to risk the pregnancy, and started his eager pursuit of the new receptionist at the office.

The afternoon that Louise finally went into labour, Colin was due at a board meeting. When she phoned his office to inform him that the baby was on the way, hoping until the last moment that he would relent and come with her to the hospital, he calmly advised her to ring for a taxi and hung up on her.

It was the sapphire-blue eyes of Mr den Haag which gazed reassuringly at her over the top of the white mask when her labour seemed to be going on for ever.

'You're not a midwife,' she managed to croak through dry lips, amazed to find the eminent paediatrician at her side.

'I was in the hospital anyway,' he soothed. 'I'll just wait with you until your husband arrives.'

'Oh, Colin won't be coming.' She couldn't completely hide her bitter disappointment. 'But you don't need to stay. I'll be quite all right.'

Nevertheless, it was his deep voice which calmed her and gave her the strength and will to keep pushing when she thought she didn't have enough energy left even to continue breathing.

And it was Mr den Haag who held her while she sobbed, broken-hearted, as he detailed the extent and the consequences of her beautiful little boy's condition.

'Because of your training you know there are various degrees of severity in spina bifida,' he had continued calmly. 'We've had a look at him. . .'

'We?' she queried, her brain slow to respond.

'Urology, orthopaedics and neurosurgery, apart from myself,' he clarified, and she nodded her comprehension of the number of disciplines involved.

'Unfortunately, there is almost total paralysis of the lower limbs and there are genito-urinary disorders involving his kidneys.'

Her tear-filled eyes were like drowned pansies looking up into the quiet strength of his face. 'So, how long do you think it'll be before he. . .' She was trying to take it as calmly as if he were just another patient, but she had never been able to stay that detached—especially now that it was her own son.

'It depends whether he gets a meningeal or ventricular infection, but as you probably know, in many cases it's loss of renal function which spells the end.'

'What about surgery? Is there no chance that. . .?' She didn't need to complete the futile hope as he shook his head then comforted her through the renewed bout of weeping.

Her despair far outweighed the comparatively meaningless outburst by her husband when he finally saw his son, and her depression became so deep that she hardly reacted at all when the policemen had come to tell her that her husband had died.

Each day, as she recovered from the traumatic birth and grew stronger, she had to watch her baby's futile struggle for life. Every few hours she would express the milk which had arrived in abundance, only to watch his feeble attempts as she encouraged him to swallow it.

Several days later—time had ceased to have any real meaning—there was a brief flurry of activity as an incubator was readied for another tiny occupant, this time a little girl.

Sitting quietly with Matthew in her arms, his dark straight hair a beautiful contrast to the honey colour of her own as she cradled him carefully against her shoulder, she overheard the nurses talking about the new arrival in hushed tones.

'Birth weight under two kilos and Apgar only six after five minutes,' she heard one mutter to the other about the baby's clinical assessment.

Never a good sign, she knew, having become accustomed to such things during her own time in this department.

The little girl was such a minute scrap of humanity as she lay in the warmth of the special incubator, all but naked to make monitoring easier. She was so much like a tiny doll that she fascinated Louise.

Over the next few hours she found herself watching the little child while she tended her own, noting with concern the increased frequency of the visits by Mr den Haag. She feared that it signalled a deterioration in the fragile baby's condition.

Perhaps it was respiratory distress syndrome due to her prematurity, although, as far as she could see, her respiration seemed within normal bounds on the monitor.

It was in the very early hours of the next morning, while she was patiently trying to persuade her own slowly weakening child to take some milk, that she became aware that someone was standing close by.

Having obtained permission to spend as much time as she needed with her ailing son, she had been so absorbed in ministering to Matthew that she had not realised that Mr den Haag had been observing for some time the tragically beautiful picture they made.

'I'm sorry. . . Oh, Mr den Haag, I didn't see you there. Is there something. . . Sister did say I could stay

with. . .' Her words tailed off as she looked closely at
his face for the first time. Initially she could hardly
believe what she was seeing, so great was the change
in him in such a few days.

Gone was the immaculately groomed consultant she
was accustomed to seeing, and there was at least a
day's growth of golden stubble on his chin, but it was
his eyes which had changed the most. Those beautiful
sapphire-blue eyes framed by startlingly dark lashes
had lost their clarity and brilliance and were now dulled
by tiredness and pain.

'I need to ask a favour from you, Mrs Roberts.'
Even his voice had a scratchy, husky quality as if it
too had lost its smoothness.

'A favour? What kind of favour?' She was mystified.
What could possibly be in her power to give to such
a powerful, eminent man?

'It's for my daughter.' He gestured briefly with one
of those elegant hands towards the little doll she had
been watching not long ago, and she understood suddenly that this was *his* child.

'She is premature, so she is very frail, and now we've
discovered that she can't tolerate cow's milk, even
when specially modified. Please——' He took a breath
and clenched his hands into fists before he continued.
'Please. She needs milk. If you could spare some. . .'
His voice stumbled to a halt as if he had no energy to
plead his case further, then he rallied before she had
a chance to speak. 'Please will you think about it?
Only, it's urgent. . .and so vital.'

His dark blue eyes blazed their full power into hers
for one stunning moment before he turned back
towards the incubator, his voice vowing huskily, 'I must
try to save her.'

He didn't stay long. Watching his tiny daughter

seemed to be destroying him, and while Louise was trying to dredge up the courage to break into the fearsome concentration he was bringing to bear on willing each new breath of life into her, he turned suddenly and strode out of the room, his face full of anguish.

Before Louise had a chance to speak to anyone about her decision, Nurse Su Yuen sped through the door her feet scarcely seeming to touch the ground.

'Louise, have you nearly finished with Matthew?' she sounded quite breathless.

'Yes, I was just about to put him down. Why? What's the matter?'

'Can you give me a hand for a few minutes? We've got one coming in on a blue light. Emergency transfer across London for the nearest bed in an SCBU.'

Louise felt the sudden familiar jump in her pulse-rate as she put Matthew in his cot.

'Right!' Her voice was brisk. 'What is it and what do we need to get ready.'

'Gastroschisis.'

'What?'

'Stomach and intestines protruding through the stomach wall. . .'

'Yes. I'm sorry, I know *what* it is—we had one delivered by Caesarean a couple of months ago. It's just that I can't believe we're seeing another one so soon.' Her hands were busy collecting and preparing the various monitoring devices which would be attached to the infant.

'Apparently, the incidence is on the increase here and in America.' Su Yuen was setting up drip stands as she spoke.

'Yes, I remember reading up about it at the time. Isn't it something like twice the number in the last five years—one in five thousand sticks in my memory?'

Louise realised that she and Su had slipped back into a smooth routine as if she had never been away. 'I can't remember if there was any reason given.'

'I can't, either. Perhaps we'll get the chance to find out when this one arrives.'

'That's a point,' Louise wondered aloud. 'Is this one a prem or what? Surely it would have been booked in for a Caesar?'

'Evidently, Mother didn't have an ultrasound scan so no one knew what was coming until it arrived.'

'Dear lord! Poor little mite. That won't have helped its chances.'

'Apparently, the midwife wrapped clingfilm around it to reduce fluid loss and risk of perforation and infection and set all the sirens going. We were the closest with room to take it.'

'God bless her for her quick thinking. She probably saved its life just with that one brainwave.'

The essential preparations completed, Su Yuen had hurried away to replenish a tray of supplies.

It was several moments before Louise remembered that she had wanted to find out how to contact Mr Den Haag to tell him his baby daughter was welcome to share her milk.

When Nurse Su Yuen came in a little while later to attend to one of the other babies, Louise impulsively broke into speech.

'Su, about Mr Den Haag's baby. . . He was saying that she needs milk. . .'

'Poor little mite. Yes, she does.' Su's face was full of compassion as she looked across at the little form in the incubator quite dwarfed by the many tubes and monitors which surrounded her. 'She had an unusually violent allergic reaction even to the specially modified milk substitutes. She's going to need a guaranteed supply of breast milk, and with her mother not about to give her any. . .'

'Not about to? What do you mean?' Louise was confused by the ambiguity. How could any mother not want to feed such a precious bundle? Was she too ill—or maybe she had no milk? Her thoughts were stopped by Nurse Yuen's words.

'Her mother died very early this morning, so they had to take the baby.'

At Louise's obvious continuing ignorance, she explained.

'The mother was in a coma after a car crash. They managed to keep her going on a ventilator for an extra week, but. . .' She shrugged to indicate the outcome, then added with some heat, 'Mr Den Haag was devastated. She was hit right outside the hospital gates by some idiot who was leaving the hospital in a tearing hurry. Well, the only place he got to in a hurry was Eternity,' she ended with a grim example of hospital humour.

She couldn't have known the chord which her narrative would strike in Louise's mind, nor the flash of understanding which would connect the whole series of random facts which caused her to draw the one inescapable conclusion: her husband, Colin Roberts, had been responsible not only for causing his own death, but also the death of Mr Den Haag's wife and the premature birth of his infant daughter.

# CHAPTER TWO

As SHE had not been expecting any visitors, Louise was once again in the special care unit with Matthew.

A woman paused, peering indecisively through the glass wall of the nursery at the two figures garbed in masks and gowns.

'There's a visitor outside the unit's doors.' Carol Long glanced up briefly. 'I wonder how she got past Sister without gowning up. Still, at least she's outside the unit itself. There'd be all hell let loose if Sister caught her in here like that.'

Louise was gently assisting Nurse Long while she removed the soiled dressings from the lesion on Matthew's back before replacing them with a fresh layer from the sterile tray beside her. Then it would be time to try feeding him again.

Obviously Mrs Roberts had recognised her daughter-in-law's easily identifiable halo of curls, because without so much as a by-your-leave she pushed open the doors bearing their 'Staff Only' message to sail into the room, her well-upholstered body clothed completely in black and her voice already chattering at full speed.

'Oh, my dear girl!' She held the handkerchief clutched in her black-gloved hand to her nose. 'What a time I've had tracking you down. They were most unhelpful on Ward Seven when I said I'd come to visit you. Told me to sit and wait while they sent a message to fetch you back from the nursery, but of course my nerves are far too bad to sit about. My Harold will be needing me in just a——Oh, my God!' Her voice rose to a breathy shriek. 'What on earth's the matter with that child's back?' Her eyes were fixed in fascinated horror on the opening at the base of Matthew's spine which was momentarily in full view before the dressing was secured in place.

'Louise, dear, I know you trained to do all this, but it's not your place to be helping the nurses with the other babies. You should have been waiting for me to visit you in the ward.' Her face showed that she was repelled by what she was seeing, but her eyes never left the tiny body.

'Still, now that I'm here you can show me my little grandson; my poor darling Colin's baby.' She finally dragged her gaze away to look around the room expectantly. 'Which one is he?'

'Mrs Roberts.' Louise's voice seemed very quiet, almost as colourless as her face in comparison with the non-stop energy of her mother-in-law's monologue as she turned the child in her arms to tuck his head into her shoulder. 'This is Matthew. My son.'

Betty Roberts' eyes bulged in horror and for a brief moment she was silent, her mouth gaping. Her make-up showed luridly as her skin turned ashen.

'Oh, no!' she wailed. 'Oh, no, no, no!' Her head was shaking wildly so that even her lacquer-reinforced hairstyle began to disintegrate, and she turned clumsily to push her way blindly through the double doors.

Louise and the nurse beside her watched in stunned fascination as the very smartly dressed middle-aged woman appeared to be doing a passable imitation of a sleepwalker as she moved down the corridor.

The door to Sister's office opened abruptly and through the insulation of the glass walls of this side of the SCBU they were witnesses to the inaudible exchange between Sister Harris and Mrs Roberts.

As they were watching, they saw Betty Roberts straighten her shoulders and plaster a smile in place before she disappeared from view through the doorway.

They looked at each other.

'My mother-in-law,' Louise confirmed, and Carol Long shrugged wryly.

Louise found that her pulse was beating in double time and her hands were trembling.

She was conscious of a feeling rather like waiting for the other shoe to drop. Betty Roberts had been badly shocked by her first sight of her grandson, especially after the death of her beloved son. But Louise knew that once she had time to think, to consider all the ramifications of the situation and consult Sister Harris about the medical facts, she would be back.

Louise had provided the milk for both of the fragile babies and she and Nurse Long were each occupied in persuading their charges to take nourishment before Betty Roberts' voice was evident again, this time from a distance as she made her subdued farewells to Sister Harris.

Transferring Matthew so that his head once more rested on her shoulder, Louise rose gently from her seat and made her way slowly towards the door, commenting quietly over her shoulder, 'I'd better keep her out of the restricted area so that she doesn't disturb the other babies or Sister Harris might think I'm more of a liability than a help and ban me from the unit.'

Closing the door behind her, she stood waiting for the approach of her mother-in-law with quiet dignity, smoothing the shock of dark straight hair on Matthew's head that was such a startling contrast to her own honey-gold fairness.

Louise knew that there was a storm brewing—she had known for the whole of the time she had carried her child that there was a chance that lightning might strike. Now it was so close that she could almost touch the electricity in the air.

'There you are, you poor dear.' As if Louise could have disappeared into thin air in the last half-hour. 'I've just been talking to that nice Sister Harris. Did you know, we were practically neighbours when we were growing up? Still, never mind that.' She straightened herself and smoothed the black satin cuffs of her jacket as if giving herself time to collect her thoughts.

'Sister Harris was just telling me about the child——' she had fixed her eyes on the fire drill instructions posted on the wall behind Louise as if her life depended on them '——and, regrettable as it is, it's better that my Colin's memory won't be living on in such a. . .' She shook her head.

'Oh, my dear, Sister told me that the child won't live very long, and with such abnormalities it's all got to be for the best. The staff here are trained to cope with such things just as much as you are, and Sister Harris said that if you wanted to come home with me now, she could ask Mr Whatever-his-name-is to send your details to our local doctor.' Her eyes flickered briefly to catch Louise's eye, but she made sure she didn't look at the child she cradled.

'I think it would be so much better if we could put all this behind us as soon as possible, and the three of us together, you, my Harold and me, can get on with making a new life. Harold and I will take care of you and help you to remember the good things.

'My Colin——' her well-endowed bosom heaved several times with an excess of emotion '——my Colin ·

was so wonderful that no one could wish such imperfection, such. . .'

'No!' Louise was suddenly a lioness defending her cub. 'Matthew is my son. I know he's desperately ill and he probably won't live very much longer, but I will not abandon him.'

Her voice was almost strident in its conviction, and so intent was she on her burning desire to safeguard her child that she didn't notice the silent figure who had just turned the corner by Sister Harris's open office door.

He had lifted a peremptory hand to prevent Margaret Harris from intervening and now paused in rapt attention at the scene being enacted by the SCBU doors.

'While he is alive, and for as long as he is alive, I will feed him and take care of him. Not because it's my duty or because he's Colin's son but because I love him.' She looked lovingly down at the frighteningly frail bundle in her arms and shifted him slightly so that she could stroke one finger gently along his downy cheek.

There was a gasping sound from Mrs Roberts as she saw the infant's face for the first time.

'Colin's son?' She gave a hysterical shriek. 'That's not my Colin's baby.' Her face was rapidly turning purple. 'You slut! You whore! How dare you try to palm some bastard off as my Colin's baby? I told my Harold you were never good enough for him!' She had to pause momentarily in her diatribe to draw another breath. 'Well, you needn't think we're going to be supporting either of you one minute longer. Oh, no!'

As she started to turn self-righteously away and leave, a further thought obviously crossed her mind so that she wheeled back to renew her attack.

'And another thing for you to think about while
you're nursing that monstrosity. When you leave here
you'll be looking for alternative accommodation,
because that house and everything in it belongs to
Harold and me, and there's no way on God's green
earth that I'll let you get your grubby fingers on one
stick of furniture or one single penny!'

With that final salvo, she turned and marched sancti-
moniously off down the corridor, passing Mr den Haag
and Sister Harris without a second glance.

Silence returned to the corridor, broken only by the
slight snuffling sound Matthew made as he fidgeted
against her shoulder.

Reflexively, Louise tightened her arms protectively
about his tiny form, conscious for the first time that
she was trembling all over. Another sound caused her
to look up in time to see Mr den Haag halt in front
of her.

'Are you all right?' His deep voice was gently solici-
tous and drew her gaze up towards his face. It was
only when she had difficulty focusing on him that she
realised that her eyes were brimming with tears.

'May I?' Two lean hands came towards her, one
offering an immaculately folded white handkerchief,
the other curved to offer to hold her baby until she
could get herself under control again.

For a second she held Matthew even tighter, her
cheek coming to rest gently on the sweetly smelling
softness of his head, before she relinquished her hold
into Mr den Haag's surprisingly expert care.

For such a large man who had apparently only
recently become a father for the first time, he was
amazingly adept at balancing Matthew's tiny form.

'Even for a paediatrician you do that very well,'
she commented, her voice husky with tears, and was

fascinated to see a dark flush wash along his high sculpted cheekbones.

'You learn many unexpected skills when you help in an orphanage,' he said gruffly before turning to hold open the nursery door for her with one broad shoulder.

That unexpected glimpse into the personal life of such an apparently private man was so fascinating that for a brief while it distracted Louise from her own problems, speculating whether he had worked in the orphanage he had mentioned as part of his training, or perhaps it had been a stint of voluntary work.

Once he had made certain that the nursery door was safely shut behind them, Mr den Haag made his way swiftly across to the incubator which still held the doll-like form of his tiny daughter, his eyes swiftly scanning the various displays which detailed the monitoring of his daughter's progress. Apparently he had completely forgotten that he still held her son in his arms.

He paused for long moments, and Louise was delighted to see his somewhat stern features gradually soften as he watched his fragile child sleeping.

While he watched, she was equally entranced to see how he had unconsciously bent his head until his lips were touching Matthew's forehead, his other hand carefully cradling the tiny head.

Briefly Louise felt the sharp pang of anguish as she realised that Matthew's own father had never held him like that, and now he never would. It was some small consolation to her that at least once in his short life her son was being held gently and apparently lovingly by a man. At least, when he was gone, she would have a mental image of what might have been.

Slowly, as if waking from a dream, Mr den Haag turned from his contemplation of his child and fixed his sapphire-blue eyes on her.

'Did you think about my request?'

For a moment she was puzzled and the emotion showed on her face.

'About the milk. . .?' he prompted.

'Oh, good lord, yes!' She hastened to reassure him. 'Ever since you asked me last night, she has been having my milk every few hours, the same as Matthew has.'

'Matthew? Which one is Matthew?' He was confused until she indicated the child he still held in his arms. 'You mean Aletta's already. . .' His pleasure changed his face completely. No longer the stern specialist or the grieving husband and father, this was a man whose face showed his delight openly so that he seemed years younger, almost boyish and so easily approachable.

When he looked like this, slightly rumpled as if it was the end of a long shift, and so much at home with the tiny child held so securely in those beautifully elegant hands, he could be just another parent sharing the triumphs and terrors of parenthood.

Their eyes met and held, deep blue gazing down into dark brown until the moment was broken by one of those funny sounds which new babies make.

'Here.' Mr den Haag turned slightly to offer her son into her care. 'Perhaps you'd better finish getting him put to bed while I do a quick check on my other tiny friends. Then, if you'll join me, I think we could both do with a cup of coffee.'

Startled, both by his suggestion and his continuing friendliness, she agreed bemusedly, and he turned and quietly left the room.

Some ten minutes later she was sitting on a straight-backed kitchen chair in the little room beside Sister's office where the nurses could grab a quick hot drink at intervals during their shift.

Mr den Haag had surprised her again by perching one hip on the corner of the table so that there were mere inches between her arm and the taut length of his thigh. For all his eminence, he seemed quite at ease with the sturdy white pottery mug full of instant coffee in his hand.

'You are Louise, yes?' It didn't happen very often as his English was so superb, but just sometimes she could detect the fact that not just his name was "foreign".

'Yes. But. . .'

He smiled almost mischievously then, and for some reason her stomach clenched in surprise at the difference that expression made.

'You might not remember, but I assisted when your baby was born.'

There was a flash of understanding in his eyes at the sadness of the resulting situation and Louise felt the ever-present tears welling up. In a hasty attempt to avoid crying all over him again, she burst into speech.

'We actually met before that, when I was working in SBCU before I left to have my baby, but when I was in labour. . .I can remember your beautiful eyes looking at me over your mask and your deep voice. . .' And she stumbled to a halt, blushing furiously at what her tongue had betrayed.

He gave an unexpected deep bark of laughter. 'Thank you for the compliment.' His eyes gleamed with his amusement at her embarrassment. 'I suppose if we're getting personal enough for compliments, I should introduce myself properly.' He slipped off the table to stand in front of her, bending forward from his great height to offer his hand.

'But I already know your name.' She was flustered by his sudden formality. 'You're Mr den Haag.'

She had been watching his face, enjoying seeing this new relaxed side to such a physically compelling man.

He reached forward to relieve her of her coffee-mug before taking her hand in his own.

'I am Jacobus Rutger den Haag, at your service.' He bowed slightly from the waist as though being formally introduced at a high society event, his accent clearly evident as he gave the first letter of his name a continental 'Y' sound, rather than the harder English 'J'. 'But my English friends call me Jacob or Jake.' This time he pronounced his name the English way.

He obviously guessed the question she hesitated to ask as he grinned again before continuing. 'I am Dutch, from den Haag—the Hague, you would call it.'

'When did you move to Britain? Your English is marvellous.'

'I learnt at school in den Haag. The Dutch as a nation are very keen on learning other languages and it was important that I did well. . .'

He seemed, for a moment as if he was going to continue speaking but then, with an almost imperceptible shake of his head, he subsided once more on to the edge of the table and leant back to brace himself on one hand.

His new position pulled his dark suit-jacket apart to display an impressive breadth of chest only thinly covered by a fine lawn shirt of a white-on-white woven design of narrow stripes.

He twisted slightly to reach out for his coffee-mug and Louise suddenly had to avert her eyes from the unexpected view of tanned naked skin overlaid by a thick golden pelt between the buttons of the front opening of his shirt. This man was her son's doctor. She should not be looking at his body like that.

She cast about rapidly in her mind for something to

say to take her mind off wondering whether his skin felt as sleek as it looked, then realised that he was speaking.

'I hadn't realised that my daughter was already receiving your milk.' Briefly his eyes swooped downwards to rest on the burgeoning fullness of her breasts, and she was startled that she seemed to feel his gaze like a physical touch, her breasts apparently growing fuller and heavier and the nipples becoming erect.

Flustered, she moved uneasily in her chair, and his eyes flicked back up to her face, his look full of unexpected knowledge, before he shuttered them with those strangely dark lashes.

'She had started receiving milk from the milk bank,' he said, and Louise blinked in confusion.

Suddenly she realised that he was referring to the system of collecting milk from mothers with excess in order to help premature babies such as his.

'It might seem selfish, but I wanted her to have milk from someone who. . .' He shook his head as his explanation faltered. 'If it was possible, I preferred to know who the milk for my baby was coming from, and once I saw you with your baby. . .'

'You mean because Matthew can't take much milk from me there would be plenty for——'

'No!' he broke in emphatically. 'No. Nothing like that.' His voice reinforced his agitated state and his gaze had become piercing as though to impress his sincerity on her.

'It was because of the way you were with your son,' he explained softly. 'Everything you do for him shows how much you love him, how much you care about him. Not every mother feels that way——' his voice became harsher '——even those with perfectly healthy babies.'

He let his eyes wander over her hair and face, his expression softening again in the way it had when he was standing beside his daughter's incubator.

'Once I had seen how gentle and loving you are to your son, I wanted your milk for my daughter.'

Her cheeks grew fiery again at the unaccustomed compliments and she sought frantically for a topic of conversation to divert him.

'What have you called her?'

He paused slightly before answering quietly. 'I have called her Aletta. It's a Dutch name. Do you like it?'

As before, when talking about matters connected with his nationality, his accent became slightly clipped. Louise found it fascinating.

'It's a beautiful name. It sounds very elegant.'

She allowed her eyes to travel the length of him from his startlingly silver-blond hair and down the breadth of his torso and the lean length of his legs before she continued thoughtfully, 'If she takes after you a bit in height, she will be tall enough to be a model.'

She smiled softly at the thought of what a daintily feminine version of the totally male being in front of her would look like. What a pity she would not be around to see if she was right.

'If she survives these first few weeks.' His tone was sombre again for a moment before lightening. 'But at least with your milk she now has the best possible chance.'

Impulsively he reached out a hand to clasp it over both of hers where they lay linked together on the table.

This time, as they touched, the sensation was almost like a low-voltage electrical charge, and they both looked at each other in surprise as they jerked apart.

Later, as Louise completed the entry in her diary she felt compelled to reveal her deepest thoughts.

Jacob—Mr den Haag—was one of the specialists I worked with in SCBU and now he's Matthew's doctor. I know it seems wrong, but somehow I feel so drawn to him. . .

# CHAPTER THREE

IN SPITE of the fact that she still spent large amounts
of time in the special nursery with Matthew, Louise
didn't see Mr den Haag for several days.

She knew from talking to the nurses that he was
visiting his daughter quite often, and on one occasion
he had even been able to feed Aletta, but it almost
seemed to Louise that he was going out of his way to
avoid seeing her. In the lonely quiet of the night she
wrote in her diary.

> Perhaps he only pretended to be friendly so that
> he could persuade me to allow my milk to be used
> for his daughter.

She was surprised how little she wanted to believe
that the man who had been so gentle with her and her
tiny son would have such a petty nature. She would
far rather suppose that he had been too busy working
to have had the time free to be in the nursery at
the same time as she was, although it was difficult
to see how. At the moment, while she was spending so much time in the unit to be with Matthew
and helping out with the other babies when an
extra hand was needed, she was probably spending
more time there than if she had been employed
full-time.

The last thing she wanted to think was that he was
deliberately avoiding her; that he might be regretting

those few seconds when his hand had touched hers and their eyes had joined in wordless communication.

When he was just five weeks old, Matthew finally lost his tenuous hold on life and, although she had known since his birth that this day would arrive, Louise was deeply shocked.

The last couple of days he had seemed to grow more fragile than ever, his skin taking on a waxy translucence, and his reactions to events around him, even to Louise herself, had been feeble.

Eventually, in spite of the fact that she had settled into a tiny bedsit just minutes away from the hospital, she had spent all of the day and most of the night at her son's bedside.

Staff Nurse Su Yuen found Louise sitting in the ward gazing blindly out of the window, her son's tiny lifeless body held gently in her arms while tears rained softly from agonised eyes to land silently on the blanket.

The quietly insistent voice finally penetrated Louise's stupor as she was persuaded to give up her fragile burden.

'Louise?' Su Yuen continued to hold her attention. 'Louise, do you want to help me take care of Matthew?'

Slowly the blank look in her sorrow-darkened eyes changed to one of puzzlement and she brushed the tears from pale cheeks with the fingers of both hands.

'Take care of him?' Her voice was hesitant. 'What do you mean? He's. . .' She couldn't bring herself to say the word yet.

'Yes. I know. But we have to take care of him for the last time, don't we?' Su Yuen paused to watch Louise's reaction closely before she made a suggestion.

'Would you like to help or would you rather I. . .?'

'No.' Louise's voice quavered but the tone was quietly determined. 'I know what to do.' And she followed her across the room without a trace of hesitation in her steps.

They had all but finished their sad task when a tiny wail sounded across the room, reminding Louise that while her own son's life had now ended, for the moment she was still necessary to the existence of little Aletta—although for how much longer, she had no idea.

Later, as Louise gave Aletta her bottle, she took comfort from the presence of the child in her arms.

The last four weeks had seen the tiny doll-like figure grow amazingly as her strength increased. Soon she would be strong enough to leave the hospital, and her need for Louise would cease when she was ready to be transferred to her father's care.

Suddenly, as if her thoughts had conjured him up, Mr den Haag pushed the doors open in time to see Louise lean forward to kiss the silky blond down on Aletta's head and stroke the velvety warmth of her cheek.

Hearing the sound of quiet footsteps approaching, Louise glanced towards their source and felt her heart leap up into her throat so that she was unable to breathe for several long moments and—'*Jacob*'—his name sounded clearly in her head.

For the first time she realised that, ever since Matthew had been born, her attraction towards Jacob den Haag had been growing. She had always respected him for the superb paediatrician he was, and had admired the compassion he had shown the parents of his tiny charges.

The last few weeks, working unofficially in the unit,

she'd had the opportunity to watch him closely at work and her admiration had only grown.

She was certain that more than one baby in the unit at present owed their lives to his swift decisiveness in acute situations, not least their newest resident who had been born just a couple of days ago at only twenty-six weeks' gestation. She glanced briefly across the room at the array of monitors surrounding her incubator. Jacob himself had nicknamed her 'the fighter' after her determined efforts to cry out her displeasure at the indignities she was suffering, in spite of her breathing difficulties.

She had survived birth and, shortly afterwards, the emergency administration of pulmonary surfactant when she developed respiratory distress syndrome, but she was still a very sick baby with a long, hard road to travel before her survival was certain.

The only regrets Louise had were that there had been no more personal contact between herself and Jacob den Haag.

His attitude had been totally correct and professional at all times—nothing at all for her to complain about.

But, a little voice whispered in her head, it would have been wonderful if only. . . But life was full of 'if only'.

If only Colin had been half the man she had fallen in love with. . .

If only Matthew had been born healthy and strong. . .

If only Aletta could be hers. . .

If only Jacob. . .

His footsteps had come to a halt and she could see the brightly polished toecaps of his shoes just a few inches away from her own much smaller feet.

She drew in a steadying breath and lifted her head to look up at him.

His stunning sapphire gaze was full of compassion and she was surprised to find it fixed, not on his daughter as she would have expected, but on her own face.

Louise was suddenly afraid that she had spoken his name aloud in her overwhelming pleasure at seeing him after so many days' absence.

A sensation of heat filled her as his gaze flickered across her eyes and down to her mouth, and she knew that she was blushing.

She was horrified that he should have seen her helpless reaction to his presence. Ducking her head down, she focused on feeding the baby the last drop of milk, wishing for the first time that, instead of her wild halo of honey curls, her hair were straight enough to swing forward so that she could hide behind it.

What kind of a mother was she, to feel such a strong attraction towards her son's doctor so soon after. . .

'Louise.' His deep voice was gentle and caused an intense reaction inside her, making her pulse beat rapidly at the base of her throat and her hands start to tremble. 'When you've finished feeding Aletta, I need to have a word with you. Would you come along to Sister's office, please?'

The words were so measured, the voice so calm, that while Louise nodded dumbly, she wondered why he should want to talk to her. He had doubtless heard about Matthew. . .

No—she shook her head silently—he would hardly need to speak to her in Sister's office just to offer his condolences. It must be. . .

'Oh, God, no! Please don't let it be that Aletta's ready to go home today. I *can't* lose them both on the same day.'

Her whispered voice was full of anguish as her arms tightened convulsively around the little girl who had come to mean so much to her; almost as much as her own son.

She automatically completed the routine of holding Aletta against her shoulder to bring up wind while her thoughts scurried around and around like panic-stricken mice.

She felt so empty, knowing that now she had no one of her own to cherish, but what would she do with herself if today was the last time she was to see Aletta?

Would she be able to bear to come back to her work in the SBCU after everything that had happened here?

Pathetic though it now seemed, she had hoped that she might have been allowed to maintain some sort of contact with Aletta, and, through her, with Jacob.

Several times over the last few days she'd had the feeling that he was watching her, and she had looked towards the glass-enclosed cubicle where the nurses could supervise the tiny ward while completing paperwork.

If he had been there, he must have hidden in the shadows, and why on earth should he do that?

During the weeks since he had helped her bring her son into the world, she had come to realise that here, at last, was someone whom she could respect. In fact, if she wasn't careful, she could easily have found herself transferring to him all the repressed emotions she longed to share.

Rousing herself out of her futile musings, she finally tucked Aletta into her cot.

'Su,' she called softly across the room to where Staff Nurse Su Yuen was suctioning her tiny charge before administering the final dose of surfactant. 'I've got to go to speak to Mr den Haag. I shouldn't be long, but do you want me to send someone in to cover for me while you're on your own?'

'Did I hear him say you would be in Sister's office?'

Louise nodded briefly, nervousness at what awaited her stealing her voice.

'I shouldn't worry, then,' Su continued. 'You'll hear the monitors in there if anything happens.'

Louise murmured her agreement and turned to leave the unit.

As her hand lifted to knock on the door, she could see that the tremor inside her was now visible, and that it increased sharply when she heard his deep voice.

'Enter.'

She took a shaky breath and complied.

Jacob, or rather Mr den Haag, she sternly reminded herself, was standing with his back towards her, gazing out of the window towards the adjacent wing of the hospital.

His elegant, long-fingered hands were clasped together to rest behind his tautly muscled hips and she was surprised to notice that his knuckles were white as if held under considerable tension.

She lifted her gaze to take in the whole of his formidably tall body and realised that his shoulders were tense too, as was the rigidly upright length of his back.

There was the sound of a deeply drawn breath and then he finally turned to face her.

He still doesn't look well, she thought instantly as she saw his pale face. Either that, or he's unhappy about something. . .

'Louise!' She jumped. By the tone of his voice it was not the first time he had spoken.

'Yes? I'm sorry. What did you say? I'm not. . .' Stop babbling! she admonished herself, and concentrated on listening to what he was saying.

'No. I am sorry. It must be difficult for you after what you've been through today. Perhaps. . .' With an air akin to relief he continued, 'Perhaps it would be better if we spoke another day.'

'Please, no!' She knew her sense was garbled but she couldn't bear to wait another day if she had to hear that the axe was about to fall.

'What did you want to say? I know you're so busy that we aren't often in the ward at the same time, so perhaps you would. . .'

If someone was going to tell her that Aletta didn't need her any more, then she would rather he was the one. At least she would have these last few moments in his company.

After today, she had so many decisions to make: about mundane things like where she was going to live, and more profound ones such as what she was going to do with the rest of her life.

At the moment she was living in a daze from hour to hour and had no answers for anything.

Even while her thoughts had buzzed around in her head unabated, her eyes had been fixed unwaveringly on the commanding figure of the man in front of her, drinking in the subtle gleam of light from the window on his uniquely silvery hair.

From her position in the little squashy chair just inside the door—she couldn't even remember sitting down in it—he seemed so large and imposing. She could see little of his expression as he was silhouetted against the window, but she saw the moment when he decided to speak.

'Firstly. . .' His voice was once again slightly accented, so she knew he was uneasy in some way. 'Let me say how sorry I am about Matthew.'

She knew from his tone that he was not just saying

the words because they were appropriate but because he genuinely meant them.

'We knew from the outset how serious his situation was, but he was as precious as any baby, and you must know that if there had been anything more we could have done. . .' He raised his shoulders and gestured with one lean hand, at a loss for further words.

'I know what you mean,' she broke in, sadly. 'I knew he couldn't survive so I tried to enjoy each moment with him. I was storing up memories of him for the future, but now that he's. . .gone. . .'

She had to draw a shaky breath before she could continue. 'I feel. . .sort of lost?'

Her questioning tone demonstrated the fact that she was trying to identify her emotions as she spoke.

'It's as if I don't really have a purpose to my life any more. At least that's the way it feels. Especially now that Aletta's so much stronger. She won't be needing me either. . .'

'Not needing you? What do you mean? What nonsense is this?' There was no hesitation in his voice now and his whole stance spoke of renewed tension.

'Well, isn't that why you wanted to speak to me? To tell me that Aletta's strong enough to go home?' She was puzzled by his apparent anger and her hands twisted together in her lap while she waited, dreading his confirmation of her worst fears.

'She has been strong enough to go home for several days now.' He had turned slightly so that she could feel the full effect of his sapphire gaze.

'What? But. . .I don't understand. If she's well enough to go home with you, why is she still here? Don't. . .don't you want to take her home?'

She was growing more confused by the minute, but her eyes never left his face.

'Of course I want to take her home with me, but I couldn't take her home because you were here with Matthew.' His answer might have been logical to himself, but certainly not to Louise.

'But what have I got to do with. . . Oh! My milk!' At last the penny dropped.

'No. At least. . . Oh, dear, this gets more complicated by the minute.' He dragged the fingers of one elegant hand through his silvery hair, leaving it endearingly ruffled, one thick strand falling forward on to his forehead to touch a startlingly dark eyebrow. 'If you will permit me to explain for a moment, and then you can ask any questions?'

Once again that delightful hint of an accent had appeared in his slightly clipped speech, and a tiny smile touched the corners of her mouth.

She had not realised that he had noticed until his silence drew her eyes upwards again and she discovered his gaze fixed on her mouth. She swallowed convulsively and the movement seemed to break the spell.

'While you were still nursing Matthew, the hospital was quite happy for Aletta to stay here as long as there was a spare cot.' He paused and tilted his head, his raised eyebrow a dark unspoken question as to whether she was following him so far.

Slightly mystified, she nodded briefly for him to continue.

'For various reasons, I would like you to continue to take care of Aletta,' he stated bluntly, then paused.

The silence started to grow while Louise tried to find the words to express her surprise, finally settling on a question.

'Various reasons? What reasons?' Perhaps while he answered she would get her euphoric thoughts organised.

He wanted her to continue to take care of Aletta! Her heart was singing at the postponement of her worst fears.

'As you know, she needs a reliable supply of milk, and as you are both the source of that supply and the closest thing she has so far known to a mother. . .' Once again that dark brow lifted quizzically and waited for her nod. 'Also, having observed you over the past weeks. . .' He paused briefly at her shocked murmur, but, when she made no attempt to speak, he continued, 'I have decided that I don't want to entrust my daughter's welfare to anyone else.'

He had finished on a triumphant note as if all was now explained to his satisfaction.

'So, for the time being, you want me to be Aletta's. . .nanny?' She tried to clarify what she had heard into the most rational meaning.

'Certainly not! That's not what I want at all!' His leanly elegant hands had clenched into powerful looking fists and his accent was growing stronger by the minute. 'You will be Aletta's mother. You understand? We must be married.'

'Married!' Louise felt all the breath leave her lungs in a rush as if she'd been punched. Her eyes opened wide, their colour deepened almost to black with shock. 'That's impossible. You can't really mean that we should get married just so that Aletta can have my milk!'

'Absolutely not,' he agreed promptly.

Louise was swept by the twin emotions of relief that she had obviously misunderstood in some way, and disappointment that he had not meant what her foolish heart had hoped.

'If it were just for milk,' he continued inexorably, 'it would be easy enough to make arrangements for a regular delivery——' he managed to make it sound like putting a note out for the milkman '—but Aletta needs someone to care for her, too.'

'I could take care of her. I'm not a trained nanny, but my hospital training would be perfectly adequate until she no longer needed me to feed her.'

'That is not enough. She needs more than that. I need more than that for her. She has lost enough,' he declared passionately.

'But I still don't see why we would have to be married.' Louise had the uncomfortable feeling that she was fighting a rearguard action. 'I could live in the house with her so she would have all the attention she needed.'

'It would not be proper,' he pronounced firmly. 'I am known in many countries and it would not be right for you to be living in the house of a man unwed.'

He was growing angry with himself at the lack of clarity of his usually impeccable speech.

Louise was torn between her amusement at this evidence that he was not as perfectly controlled as he would like, and blind panic as she realised how determined he was to have his own way.

'And is it proper for two people who have each only just lost their partners to be contemplating marriage again so soon?' she counter-attacked wildly.

'What business is it of theirs?' His bluntness bordered on arrogance. 'They do not know why we will make our decision.'

He was still for several moments, his gaze fixed on her face as if he wanted to strip her soul bare.

'May I be brutally frank with you, Louise? You will not take offence?'

Louise gestured with an open palm for him to continue.

'Neither of us made a good choice of partner at our first attempt. From what you have said, it would seem that your Colin was a selfish philanderer who only married you to please his father and produce a child with the added bonus of titled connections.'

He had said he would be brutal and he certainly wasn't pulling any punches.

'My choice was no better,' he continued, the bitterness of disillusionment tingeing his voice. 'My wife was a career-woman who didn't want a husband so much as she wanted a career asset.'

He straightened to his full height and took a deep, cleansing breath.

'At least the two of us will be honest with each other as to the reasons why we will marry.' His tone had softened, become more persuasive. 'It will be for Aletta, for propriety and perhaps, a little, for companionship?'

Before she could gather her thoughts he continued softly, 'or is it that you do not wish to care for my Aletta?'

His attack was sly and his aim was true.

'No. . .yes. . .oh! Of course I do.' There was no way she could deny it. 'But that doesn't mean that we should——'

'You would have her grow up with a mother and father who are not married?' He renewed the assault before she could attempt to marshall her forces, but the words he used brought an automatic disclaimer.

'But I'm not her mother!'

'Yes, you are,' he countered. 'As much as, if not more than the woman who carried her in her body and had to be bribed to have her!'

For long moments his harsh voice echoed in the

shocked silence, and her eyes grew huge in her
pale face.

'She wanted to. . .' Words failed her as she shook
her head in denial.

'She cared more for the money she could make by
removing double chins from overweight society
matrons and inflating the figures of simpering models
than carrying and giving birth to her. . .my child.' His
words halted as he brought both hands up to rub
harshly at his face as if he wanted to erase the
memories.

'It was only when I begged—yes, begged her not to
abort my child that she finally relented, but only on
condition that once the child was born she was to have
no responsibility for its welfare.'

He slowly shook his head at the memory of his wife's
implacable terms. 'At least I wasn't rejected until *after*
I was born.'

His final words were spoken in such a low voice
that Louise was almost certain that he was unaware of
uttering them, but, for all their softness, their effect
was shattering.

At a stroke, Louise had been granted a totally
unexpected insight into the private torments of Jacob
den Haag.

'That is not true of Aletta,' she reminded him, drawing him out of his less than happy memories. 'She will
always know that you love her.'

'Yes.' His face softened. 'Even before I knew
whether she was girl or boy, it didn't matter. It was
enough just that she existed.' He shook his head.
'Then, when I nearly lost her. . .'

'I'm so sorry,' Louise broke into the remembered
heartache. 'It was all my fault.'

'Your fault? Not so? It was that idiot. . .'

'My husband.' Her voice was bleak. 'If it weren't for my family history, it would never have happened, but I didn't know. . .'

'No! It was not your fault,' he interrupted forcefully. 'You were not driving the car. He was. It was his fault, and his alone.'

'You don't blame me?' Her voice was hesitant but her eyes were filled with torment.

'It never occurred to me to blame you.' He spoke with simple honesty. 'You are the one who made my daughter grow well and strong; the one who shows her what a mother's love feels like, who comforts her when she is unhappy, who takes care of her. You are the most important person in her universe.' His gaze was direct and totally without artifice.

Suddenly, his insistence on the stability of marriage between the two of them started to make sense, even if the only person to benefit was his tiny daughter.

But what of her own emotions?

She already loved Aletta, as he did, but what of love for herself? Was there never to be someone to love her alone? Someone strong and steadfast whom she would love in return? Someone like. . .?

Such thoughts were dangerous. They would undermine the agreement Jacob was suggesting between them. But oh. . .if only. . .

'Yes,' she said simply, before her wishes and daydreams could overtake common sense.

'Yes?' he queried. 'Yes to what?' His eyes were fixed on her face, their colour deeper than ever.

'Yes, I will marry you.' The words were scarcely more than a whisper but he heard.

Both hands reached out to capture hers and draw her towards him. She felt the smooth-roughness of his jacket against her hands as he held them to his chest.

'Thank you,' he murmured. 'For myself and for
Aletta, thank you.' And he leant forward to place a
kiss on her forehead.

# CHAPTER FOUR

ONCE Louise had agreed to his proposal, events started to move with frightening speed, almost as if Jacob was afraid she would change her mind.

Several times during the next few days she found herself going over their conversation, and each time she winced when she remembered how he had stressed that their relationship would be based on honesty.

She knew, now, that she had not truly been honest with him because she had not been honest with herself.

It was only in the quiet darkness of the night, when she returned to snatch a few hours' sleep in her dreary little flatlet, that she had finally admitted the shameful truth to herself.

In the few short weeks since Colin's death she had grown far more attracted to Jacob than she had ever been towards her husband.

Gradually her mental discomfort grew until it had blossomed into full-blown panic. Her pen flew over the page of her diary.

What on earth am I doing? We know so little about each other. We must be fools to think it can work. What if he falls in love with someone? Would he make me go—make me leave Aletta? What if I fall in love with him?

Jacob had organised the ceremony for the first available day and had arranged for Aletta to remain at the hospital until then, although the tiny girl no longer needed nursing.

Louise had realised immediately that to spend the next few days in her cramped little flatlet with nothing to think about other than walking to the hospital to provide Aletta's next feed—and worrying about the step she would be taking in the frighteningly near future—would send her swiftly mad.

She had approached her superiors with the offer of working in SCBU on a voluntary basis until Aletta left, and found herself not only welcomed with open arms but put on the temporary payroll as well.

'My dear, you're a godsend,' Sister Wilson had said. 'You know as well as I· do how few SCBUs there are in the country, and it takes a special type of person to cope with the stress. Losing you is going to be a big blow, so we're glad to hang on to you for as long as we can!'

Louise had blushed and stammered her thanks, glad to be able to keep frantically busy for as much of the day as possible and grateful beyond words that she had not been grilled about the earth-shattering event which would take place in just a few days. She could only suppose that Jacob had made all the necessary explanations.

With two new patients admitted within hours of each other, one before and after reconstructive heart surgery and the other another prem with breathing difficulties, they were kept at full stretch, with visits from the paediatric anaesthetist and surgeon to organise while calming frantic relatives.

Of course, she had seen Jacob. Quietly and calmly he had gone about his work as proficiently as ever, sending a brief glance her way as he sailed into the unit to confer with his colleagues or check up on one of his little charges.

Several times they had rubbed shoulders while tending to their patients, trying to insert a frighteningly long catheter into veins which seemed too fragile to stand the procedure.

'I've always hated holding them down like this.' The words were out of her mouth before she realised.

Jacob's eyes met hers over the tops of their masks but there was no censure in them.

'It is better this way.' His deep voice was slightly muffled as he leant forward again to begin.

'I know,' she sighed as she held the little body firmly, one finger stroking the skin reassuringly. 'It would be so dangerous if he wriggled at the wrong moment, but it seems so cruel, somehow, when they're already having so many problems. I just want to cuddle them and promise it will all go away. . .' She bit her lip as she realised how she was babbling on.

'That's what makes you so good with the patients.' His voice was pitched softly as he concentrated. 'You are excellent at your job, but because you care about the patients as individuals, they seem to pick it up and respond to it. . .' His words tailed off as he checked the placement of the catheter, having inserted it right up to the tape marker.

'There we go.' He straightened up, his eyes smiling at her over the top of his mask. 'A successful bit of threading there. I'll be well in practice if Aletta needs laces or elastic in a few years!'

It had been the only time the future had been mentioned between them in the run-up to their wedding-day, as he had immediately reverted to giving instructions for the continued care of their patient.

It was her off-duty time, when there was nothing

more to do but stare at the ceiling and try to sleep when all her doubts came back to plague her, and the more she thought, the more she became convinced that the whole idea was impossible.

Finally, on the morning of their wedding, she could stand it no longer and tried to contact Jacob to tell him she couldn't go through with it.

'I'm sorry, Mrs Roberts,' his secretary confirmed for the third time, 'I can't seem to contact Mr den Haag at the moment. Are you sure you don't want to leave a message for him?'

'Would you tell him. . .?' What? Tell him she wouldn't be marrying him today? That would be all around the hospital grapevine before she'd put the phone down.

'No.' Her tone was resigned. 'No message.'

By quarter-past eleven she was stepping out of the taxi he had organised. Her ivory silk dress and jacket seemed to shimmer as she slowly climbed the steps towards the imposing wooden door and the sun came out at last from behind the clouds.

She was one step from the top when the door opened and Jacob appeared. Stunned by the power of his presence, she was unable to move until he stepped forward and offered her his hand.

Louise had tried to ignore the electricity which seemed to flow between the two of them, had tried to believe that it was just a faulty memory of a time when she was under great stress.

The first touch of his hand on hers proved that she was wrong. The charge was stronger than ever, and, as he linked his fingers between hers to guide her through the door, she felt a fine tremor start deep inside.

'Here.' He paused just inside the door to show the contents of his other hand. 'They go with your outfit. . .and with you.' And he handed her a perfect spray of orchids.

The blooms were the colour of rich cream, shaded towards their centres with tones of honey and deep sherry-gold, the frilled outer edges accented with a deeper bronze.

'Oh, Jacob, they're beautiful,' Louise breathed as she felt the hot prickle of tears behind her eyes. 'I didn't expect. . .'

'It was my pleasure.' He gave a courtly bow before bending towards her. 'There is a pin, if you will permit me to help?'

Inexplicably, Louise felt all her fears melting away. Perhaps it was the clipped lilt to his voice, betraying the fact that he, too, was nervous. Perhaps it was the sight of the startlingly dark lashes fanning over the smoothly tanned planes of his cheekbones as he concentrated on pinning the corsage in place. Perhaps it was the corsage itself—not only the fact that he had thought to give her one to make the day special, but that he had chosen one to suit her colouring so well.

Whatever the reason, she was filled with new strength, a new resolution that the step they were taking today was the right one for both of them.

The chilly formality of the waiting-room was much as she had expected, right down to the imitation silk flowers. Her quiver of apprehension at meeting his guests was stilled by the shock of finding the room completely empty.

She sat numbly in the enervating silence. Hadn't he invited anyone to his wedding? He knew that she had been unable to contact her mother in time and her grandparents had declined to travel to London for the event in spite of Jacob's offer of transport and hotel accommodation. But what about his family?

'Was there not enough time for your family to come over?' The words burst out of her, carried on a wave of old feelings of inadequacy.

'Come over?' His eyes were as strangely wary as his tone.

'From Holland,' she clarified. 'Should we have allowed them more time so they could be here?'

'No.' He sounded resigned. 'Timing wasn't a factor. . .'

A voice from the doorway interrupted to call them through to the other room.

'But who will be our witnesses if neither of us has any family here?'

'Don't worry about it.' He sounded far calmer than she felt. 'They are well used to organising two witnesses if couples come without any of their own.'

Sure enough, two clerical staff were co-opted into the proceedings, and Louise couldn't help but feel that the whole event had a slightly surreal air about it.

Right up to the moment when the registrar's voice told Jacob he could kiss his bride Louise had the strange feeling that she must be dreaming. Then his large warm hands took hold of her shoulders and turned her towards him, the thick strand of silver-blond hair falling forward to touch his peculiarly dark eyebrows as he leant towards her.

His lips felt strangely cool as they touched hers for the first time, the contact infinitely gentle—but the impact on her senses held Louise in thrall.

Her eyes closed, her very stillness making her more aware than ever of the masculine scent of his skin surrounding her, overpowering her as he himself was, his sheer size cutting her off from the rest of the world.

Her pulse quickened slightly as she fought to contain the panic which started to grow. He was so big, so powerful, like a force of nature in his contained immobility.

She hadn't realised that her lips had parted in an unconscious gasp until she felt the probing warmth of his tongue, the contact shocking in its novelty. Before she could think about complaining that this was not in their agreement, Jacob angled his head to align their mouths even more closely and Louise ceased to think at all.

All her senses focused on his stunning possession of her, his arms wound firmly around her, holding her slender body against the broad power of his, her feet scarcely touching the floor. His tongue, too, had taken possession, filling her mouth with gentle mastery and a host of sensations she had never dreamt were possible.

The sound of a polite cough intruded, drawing Louise back to reality with a vengeance. Mortified by her lack of control, she drew her hands away from their preoccupation with the silky profusion of the hair at the back of his neck, her cheeks burning as she fixed her gaze on the subdued pattern of his tie, totally unable to meet his eyes.

'Er—congratulations, Mr and Mrs den Haag.' The registrar's voice was an inconsequential murmur in the background, Louise's ears filled with the simultaneous baritone rumble of Jacob's voice.

'Congratulations, Mrs den Haag.' His breath puffed softly over her face as he spoke, one hand coming up to raise her chin.

She looked up briefly, afraid that her stunned vulnerability would be all too visible in her eyes. The gentle understanding on his face calmed her fears, and when one arm encircled her shoulders and turned her to face the patiently smiling registrar she found herself able to make her thanks quite composedly.

They emerged into the brightness of the day and Louise felt her heart sink. Her brief time with Jacob was at an end. The hospital would claim him now. There was no reason for her to feel disappointed— she knew well enough from talking to the partners of other specialists what life would be like married to such an eminent man.

She stood quietly at his side, revelling in the closeness brought about by the arm which still curved around her while he hailed a taxi.

'The Royal, please,' he directed when they were settled.

'What. . .? But. . .aren't you due back at the hospital?' Her spirits lifted at this unexpected turn of events.

'Not yet,' he answered firmly, taking her hand in his. 'I thought it would be appropriate for us to share our first meal together before the outside world intrudes?' His tone was questioning. 'Unless you would prefer that we go to the hospital to pick up Aletta?'

'No. Er—yes. . .' She stammered to a halt.

'So decisive,' he mocked gently.

'We can collect Aletta, if you want to, but. . .' She glanced quickly at his face, attracted again by its lean perfection. 'But I would like to eat.' She dropped her gaze to their linked hands and squeezed experimentally. 'I'm starving,' she confided.

His burst of full-throated laughter drew an answering smile.

'Didn't you have breakfast this morning?' he quizzed.

'No. There were too many butterflies in there.'

He stilled. 'It's too late now, you know.'

There was a rough edge to his voice.

'Too late for what?'

'To change your mind.'

Startled, she looked straight at him.

'That *was* why you were trying to contact me this morning, wasn't it?' His sapphire gaze pierced her to the core and she caught sight of a fleeting vulnerability.

Suddenly, she understood. He had thought she was going to reject him.

'Yes. . .no.'

'Oh, dear. Back to that.' His expression was wry. 'Which one is it? Yes, or no?'

'Both.' She was blunt.

'Oh, come on. . .!'

'Yes, I did have second thoughts about marrying you.' She paused as his face closed up on her. 'I'm still not happy about marrying you so cold-bloodedly.' She paused, uncertain how to continue.

'Hardly cold-bloodedly, after that kiss in the register office.' His deep voice was husky and she felt the heat flooding her cheeks.

'Yes, well, it must have been the tension of the occasion.'

'Maybe,' he allowed wryly. 'But what about your second thoughts?'

'In the end I realised that even though it was just a marriage of convenience for us, it means much more than that to Aletta.'

'Ah, yes. Aletta.' He sighed deeply. 'Well, if we both keep her firmly in mind, everything should sort itself out.'

Louise would have liked to ask why he seemed suddenly subdued—surely she had given the answer he wanted?—but the taxi drew up outside the Royal just then, and the opportunity was lost.

Their meal was a low-key affair. Louise was glad he

had thought to arrange it, although the atmosphere was rather strained at first.

By the time they were drinking their second cup of coffee at the end of a sumptuous meal she realised that they had started to regain the easy manner which they had achieved at the hospital.

She grew pensive as she remembered the mugs of coffee they had drunk while they chatted in the small hours of the night when both their babies had been so ill. They had spoken more openly then, had been less wary of each other.

'A penny for your thoughts?' His smooth baritone interrupted her musings.

'Nothing worth that much, I'm afraid,' she dismissed quietly. 'I was just thinking about those long nights at the hospital.'

'When you were nursing?'

'No. After Matthew was born.'

'It will take you some time to get over a tragedy like that.' He hesitated, fixing her with his serious gaze for long moments before he spoke again. 'If it will help you, please, talk about him.'

She made a small startled sound but he continued.

'I knew him too, and I won't mind. It's better than locking it all inside, the way you do.'

'I do?' She sounded startled.

'We both tend to keep things to ourselves,' he confirmed. 'It's probably because we're rather solitary. Isn't it strange,' he mused, idly, 'how two people brought up in such different surroundings can turn out so similar.'

He glanced briefly at his watch and Louise suddenly realised how long they had taken over their meal.

'Is it time to collect Aletta?'

'It would be a good idea, then we can get her

settled down before I give you a guided tour of the house.' And he signalled for the bill and asked for a taxi.

Their arrival at the hospital to collect Aletta went beautifully smoothly right up to the moment when Jacob's pager sounded its summons.

'One of these days I'll work out how they manage to find out when I'm in range,' he muttered ruefully as he made for the nearest phone only to return almost immediately.

'I'm sorry, Louise. There's a baby coming straight up. Mother's been on methadone and the baby's having seizures. Dammit.' He turned away violently, swearing for the first time in Louise's hearing. 'Why won't they realise that methadone addiction is even more severe for the baby they're carrying than heroin.' His fists clenched and released rhythmically as he contained his anger.

'I can take Aletta home if someone can organise some transport,' she offered calmly. 'Then you won't be worried about us waiting here.'

'Are you sure?' He raked his fingers through the escaping lock of hair to restore his habitual neatness. 'It certainly makes more sense, although I had intended taking you there for the first time. . .' His attention was drawn by the soft chime announcing the arrival of the lift.

'How will we get in the house?' Louise's words caught him as he turned to walk towards it.

'Here.' He retrieved a set of keys from his pocket and separated one to hand it to her. 'My secretary can call for transport and get someone to help you carry everything.' He glanced across at the emerging gurney then touched her shoulder briefly. 'I'll be home as soon as I can. I'm sorry about this,' he gestured.

'It's not a problem.' She smiled to reassure him, squashing down her own disappointment. 'It's all part of the job, isn't it?' And she watched as he turned away from her to approach his tiny patient.

Her arrival at the smart London townhouse she would now be living in was something of an anticlimax after the eventful day so far.

Aletta had been a little angel and the driver had been well tipped to carry several bulky packages up the steps for her.

Once she was finally alone, Louise stood in the hallway with Aletta in her arms and gazed around her.

The house was deceptive. From the outside it seemed quite compact, but once inside it was amazingly spacious, with a flight of stairs rising from the other end of the entrance hall towards a large window framed by Wedgwood-blue curtains.

Louise wandered through the ground floor, marvelling at the welcoming atmosphere. There was no sign of Jacob's impoverished childhood in the quiet good taste of the furnishings, and she was forced into an uncomfortable comparison with her own childhood home.

She had been brought up in the manor which had been in her family for several generations but, for all that it was filled with numerous heirlooms, it had never given her the same sense of 'coming home' that Jacob had achieved.

The same air of comfort and quiet good taste continued in the rooms upstairs as she wandered from one to the other, finally finding herself in Aletta's nursery.

She knew without asking that the design of this room

had been his own, there were so many individual touches. The mural on the wall beside her cot was filled with the nursery rhyme characters of Jack and Jill, but in this case there was a windmill on the hill and they were each dressed in traditional Dutch costumes.

Louise smiled.

'Aletta, my little love, you don't know how lucky you are to have a Daddy who loves you so much,' she murmured softly to the sleeping infant before tucking her down in her new cot until she was ready to wake for her next feed.

She had unpacked her belongings into the single room adjoining one side of Aletta's nursery and had marvelled at the beautiful selection of clothing ready for Aletta as soon as she grew big enough. The enormous number of toys made her smile again. They were proof, if further proof was needed, that Jacob was besotted with his tiny daughter.

Aletta had woken slightly earlier than usual for her feed—hardly surprising after the upheaval of the day.

Louise had just collected the bottle from the kitchen and was carrying Aletta towards the stairs when she became aware that she was not alone.

For a moment she stood completely still, the perfect replica of a Madonna with Aletta lying peacefully in her arms, while all her senses searched for clues.

It was not until a slight sound drew her eyes upwards that she saw the figure silhouetted against the window at the turn of the stairs.

'Jacob.' It was hardly more than a whisper and far too quiet for him to have heard, but he had obviously watched her mouth form the word.

'Louise.' His voice, too, was gentle, the deep richness of it reaching her as he came down the staircase towards her.

Long seconds passed while she tried to persuade her limbs to move, but it was not until the child in her arms moved fretfully that she even remembered her burden.

'How is everything? Any problems?' His eyes were never as blue as this in her memories, were they? He came to a halt in front of her, that quizzical eyebrow once more aloft and a gentle half-smile on his lips.

'Aletta's been fine.' She didn't understand how she could be conducting a rational conversation when just the scent of his body was short-circuiting her senses. 'In fact she slept all the way here. She's only just woken up for her feed.'

She felt her cheeks grow fiery as she realised that his eyes had never left her.

'Do you want to hold her?' She offered up the warmly clad little bundle. 'She won't mind waiting a few minutes for her feed.'

He shook his head and a lock of silvery hair fell forward.

'Before I do anything else, I need to take a very long, hot shower.' He reached out one elegant finger and stroked the downy baby cheek which was almost all that he could see of her. 'You carry on up to the nursery and I should feel a little more presentable by the time you've finished.' Midnight-dark lashes lifted suddenly and she was mesmerised by sapphire-blue lasers.

Deep inside her she felt a slow, insidious heat start to burn, and when his head dipped forward to deliver the gentlest of kisses to her startled lips she gave an astonished gasp at the resulting sharp twist of excitement.

He had straightened immediately as she tried to cover her reaction, but she was afraid that he had seen the telltale signs of her almost instant arousal all too clearly.

She had changed Aletta and was just about ready to give her the bottle when Jacob came into the nursery clad only in a navy Paisley-patterned robe in a heavy silky fabric.

Her eyes travelled from the silvery hair, still darkened several shades by his shower, over his freshly shaved jaw and down his chest to the V of tanned flash revealed by his robe. The hem stopped just below mid-thigh—perhaps because he had difficulty finding clothes suited to his stature—and his elegant feet were as bare as his hair-sprinkled legs.

He paused just inside the room, a frown pulling his dark brows together as he pushed the door closed behind him.

'Are you not feeding Aletta yourself?' The words emerged abruptly, tinged with an emotion which Louise was unable to identify.

'You can feed her if you like.' She smiled, holding out the bottle towards him as he prowled forward.

'No, that is not what I meant.' As ever, his speech became clipped and he drew in a sharp breath, demonstrating his exasperation with himself. 'I will start again, and this time I will be more precise.

'Aletta is still receiving your milk, I know, but why do you not feed her yourself? Do you not want her to feed from you?' His hands made an explicit cradling motion and her sudden comprehension made her blush to the roots of her hair.

'No. Yes. I mean, I don't. . .I haven't. . .' To her embarrassment she felt a prickling behind her eyes as if tears were imminent.

'Louise, Louise.' He almost crooned her name as he stroked one hand gently over the silky halo of her

hair. 'I did not mean to upset you with my clumsiness.'
He slipped one finger under her chin and exerted just
enough pressure to raise it until her drowned pansy
eyes reluctantly met his. 'I wanted to know if you
preferred to feed Aletta this way. I did not know if
you had tried. . .' He allowed his words to die on a
questioning note.

'I didn't try because. . .well, partly because I
didn't know if you wanted me to. . .' She paused
uncertainly.

'Ah! Louise. I would be delighted—if that's what
you would like? I know you weren't able to feed
Matthew, and it's possible that after all this time Aletta
will not want to change her routine.' He hesitated,
and then proved his sensitivity beyond doubt when he
quietly asked, 'Would you prefer me to leave, or would
you welcome my assistance?'

For long moments Louise was struck dumb by the
force of the twin emotions which assailed her, her
self-consciousness warring with the strength of her
desire for such an intimacy with him.

'Please. Stay.' Shyness made her voice almost inaudible but the emotion had not been the victor.

Louise was relieved when Jacob calmly took Aletta
from her while she attempted to loosen her clothing.
When her dress proved unsuitable, he disappeared
briefly, his little daughter cradled safely in the crook
of one strong arm, to return with one of his towelling
robes which he suggested she use.

Gently he settled Aletta into her arms when she was
once again ensconced in her nursing chair and knelt
down by her side. The unexpected view of the naked
breadth of his chest revealed as he leant towards her
made her heart leap into her throat, the roaring in her
ears almost drowning out the sound of his voice.

'She is accustomed to the feel of the synthetic nipple, so she will need your nipple to mimic the stiffness.' His voice was as unemotional as if he was lecturing to a group of colleagues, and left Louise gazing at him blankly.

'Here. If you will allow me to. . .' The rest of his words were lost as her ears were filled again with the sudden pounding of her heartbeat as, for the first time, his hand touched her breast.

She was utterly stunned as she felt him take her nipple between his finger and thumb, the sensation dragging her gaze down to view the startling contrast of the bronzed elegance of his hand against the creamy ivory of her swollen breast.

She gave an audible gasp of dismay as he squeezed the nipple gently and twisted it. Her eyes flew up to meet his as she felt the answering twist of arousal deep inside her body and she caught a glimpse of a momentary flash of fire in his widely dilated pupils before they were quickly shuttered.

'Look.' He redirected her attention to her breast by slipping his fingers underneath it to cup it in his palm. 'See how the nipple is ready to be suckled.' His tone had deepened and his words had become slightly slurred as if he was having some difficulty speaking, and he paused briefly to swallow.

'Now,' he murmured, 'we will see if Aletta will accept the changed packaging of her meal.' The humour was slightly forced, but Louise was grateful for the attempt.

In the event, Aletta needed very little persuasion before she accepted Louise's nipple, and for the first time she knew the singular joy of suckling a baby at her breast. She was so wrapped up in the new sensations that it was several moments before she realised that Jacob still held her breast cupped in the warmth of his palm.

Glancing quickly up at him, she saw that he too was entranced, watching his little daughter feeding. When he lifted his suspiciously bright eyes to meet hers, the breath caught in her throat at the fact that he should make no attempt to hide his emotion from her.

His fingers tightened briefly, reminding her anew of the position of his hand, and she became rather flustered as she tried to find the words to draw the fact to his attention. She should have known he would dispense with her shyness.

'Would you rather I didn't touch your breast?' His directness took her breath away, and she was unable to answer. 'If you wish, I will take my hand away, but I wanted—no, I *need*—to feel that I am taking part, that I am sharing. . .'

And, just like that, all embarrassment was gone.

As soon as she remembered how little he had been allowed to share in the magic of waiting for his child to be born, Louise's heart went out to this gentle giant of a man and she realised again how much she was beginning to care for him.

'No. I don't mind,' she acquiesed softly, and stifled the little voice inside her which would have given a far less equivocal answer.

It was not until Aletta had been put to bed that Louise's euphoric mood was shattered.

She had been mentally perusing the contents of her wardrobe for items of clothing which would make feeding Aletta easier, but when she crossed the soft green carpet of the single room next to the nursery to look, the wardrobe was empty.

She stood for a moment, puzzled. Had she only

imagined unpacking her cases? She turned to the other cupboard to look for them, but they were missing, too.

'Jacob?' she called quietly from the doorway just as he came out of Aletta's room.

'Yes?' As he turned towards her, still wearing the softened look he always had when he was with his daughter.

'Do you know what has happened to my cases—and my clothes. I was sure I had unpacked them, but. . .'

'I moved them.' His voice was quietly firm.

'Oh. I'm sorry. I presumed this room would be the most convenient for looking after Aletta, but if you would prefer. . .'

'I have moved them into our room.' He indicated the door on the other side of Aletta's room.

'Our. . .?' She was unable to continue. All the air had left her lungs in a rush.

For several seconds there was a deafening silence as the implication swept over her, then anger rushed through her in a deluge.

'And who gave you the right to do that?' Her voice throbbed with emotion as she felt the heat of embarrassment scorch her cheeks.

'You did.' By comparison, he seemed utterly calm. 'This morning, when we were married.'

'But that was for Aletta's sake. It's a marriage of convenience. We agreed.'

'Yes, we agreed.' At his calm confirmation she took a quick breath of relief, then he continued. 'We agreed it would be for Aletta's sake. That she should grow up in a normal family atmosphere with a father and a mother.'

Her pulse-rate had dropped nearly back to normal and she felt the hectic flush calming down.

'Tell me,' he posed conversationally, 'how many chil-

dren have parents who sleep in different rooms? How
normal do you think that is going to seem to her?'

'But it's not that sort of marriage,' she wailed helplessly, horrified at how much she was beginning to wish
it were. 'How can we sleep in the same bed if we're
not. . .?' In spite of her years of nursing she found
herself unable to continue. The heat rose again in her
cheeks as her eyes travelled defencelessly over his
taut body.

'Do you think I'm some sort of animal?' he
demanded, and she was sure she detected hurt in his
tone. 'Just because I'm strong, it doesn't mean that I
would force myself on you. I am well able to control
myself—I have done for years.'

There was definite bitterness in his final words so
that Louise found herself wondering at the cause. Was
it her mistrust, understandable though it might be, or
was it an older hurt that haunted him?

It was his determined attempt to hide his past hurts
from her which calmed her fears.

'Well,' she started uncertainly, 'if you really think
it would be best for Aletta. . .'

'It would,' he broke in decisively as her words faded.
'We are both sensible adults. We can work any problems out as they come along.'

'I would rather we made it a sort of trial run,' she
suggested, her voice sounding far calmer than she
felt inside. 'Then, if it's not working out, we can
think again.'

'Fine,' he agreed shortly, stepping back to gesture
her towards the room.

She hesitated, still uncomfortable with the idea of
sharing such intimate space with him while he was still
dressed only in a short silky robe.

'I'll need to put my things away—or should I cook

something?' Her tawny eyes looked even larger in the pinched nervousness of her face.

'I'll go through to the bathroom to dress.' How had he known that the sight of so much naked tanned male flesh was making her nervous? 'Then I need to check through my post and see if there are any messages on the answering machine. If you want to unpack, you will see where the empty drawers and cupboards are, but you won't need to cook. Everything is already prepared and won't take long to be ready.'

'It is?' She couldn't help sounding surprised. 'Who did the preparation? Do you have someone who comes in?' How little they knew of each other's lives.

'No. *I* did it.' There was an endearing hint of colour along the lean plane of his cheeks. 'I wanted to welcome you to your new home, and our new life, with a special meal.'

'You cook, too?' She couldn't help teasing him a little. 'I've married a paragon of all the virtues.'

'Not *all* the virtues,' he denied, deadpan, but he couldn't hide a gleam in his eyes.

'Yes, well,' Louise retreated, nervous tension catching at her again. 'If you sort out your paperwork, I'll put my things away.'

Although he complied readily enough, she heard a quiet chuckle as he walked towards the bathroom.

They spent a pleasant evening together, first over a beautifully prepared meal, then in the lounge where they watched a disturbing documentary about third-world poverty which sparked a lively debate between them.

Louise was amazed that on the surface they seemed as relaxed and comfortable with each other as if they had been married for years, but little things belied the fact—a casual glance caught and held just those few beats too long, and the accidental contact which caused each of them to move apart just a little too quickly.

Gradually, over the space of the evening, the tension grew inside her until she felt that at the least thing she would shatter like spun glass.

A phone call from the hospital giving the update he had requested on his various small patients gave Louise the chance to slip upstairs to give Aletta her last feed. She had been worried that she couldn't cope with the intimacy if Jacob wanted to help her the way he had earlier. It had affected her emotions so deeply that another taste of his gentle ministrations just before they went to bed together would make nonsense of their agreement.

Never mind worrying that Jacob might act like an animal and force himself on her, she was in danger of leaping on him. Now, there was a case for equality!

She had just finished feeding Aletta when Jacob arrived in the nursery, and she was gratified to see his open disappointment.

'Do you want to give her a cuddle in case she's still got any more wind?' Louise offered, and was rewarded with a heartwarming smile.

'I'd love to.' He walked towards her, his long legs covering the distance swiftly. 'Hello, precious,' his voice was gentle as he leant towards his little daughter.

Louise went to pass her into his arms, but he fore-stalled her, sliding his hands around her to support her head and bottom.

The contact between the back of his hand and her breast might have been purely accidental, but the acute twist it gave to her awareness of him made her draw in a sharp breath.

He froze in position. 'Did I hurt you?' he asked quickly.

'N . . .no,' she stammered, helplessly glancing down to where his hand was still in contact with her sensitive nipple.

He followed her gaze then looked up at her in time for her to see his pupils dilate as he realised what had happened. Sapphire-blue darkened to midnight and left her feeling helpless to break the contact.

Long seconds later he shakily drew in a deep breath and lifted Aletta out of her arms.

'If you want to use the bathroom first——' his baritone voice was decidedly husky '—I'll put Aletta to bed.' And he finally released her gaze as he turned away.

'Right,' she whispered faintly, and fled from the room.

As she slipped under the edge of the covers, she was sure she had never prepared for bed so fast in her life.

She had left the small light burning on the cabinet on Jacob's side of the bed, but her own was in darkness when she finally heard the sound of keys being removed from a pocket and placed on the dressing-table.

For such a big man, she thought, bemusedly, he moves almost as quietly as one of the great cats.

The endless moments while he was in the bathroom were spent fruitlessly trying to force herself to relax enough to go to sleep.

When she finally felt the other side of the bed dip under his silent weight, the surprise nearly made her leap out of her skin.

'Louise. . .' The warm hand on her shoulder urging her to turn towards him made her stiffen in panic, her eyes huge and dark in a pale face.

'You. . .you said we wouldn't. . .' she stumbled breathlessly.

'I know,' he said gently, a strange sadness in his voice. 'I just wanted to say goodnight.' And he leant over her, the breadth of his naked shoulders blocking the light completely so that his face was in shadow.

The warmth of his lips pressed against her forehead for a brief fraction of a second and then was gone as he angled his head to brush the lightest of kisses over her mouth.

'Sleep well.' His breath was minty as it puffed gently over her face and teased the curls at her temples, then he turned away from her and pulled the covers up over his shoulder. Within minutes he was deeply relaxed, his breathing slowing into sleep.

If that's what I was worried about, she thought to herself, I wasted a great deal of nervous energy over nothing, and she turned away from him, totally disgruntled.

But, as she mentally replayed that final scene and recalled the butterfly delicacy of the contact between their lips and the surge of pleasure it had caused, a little mental voice queried insistently, Nothing?

# CHAPTER FIVE

I am now Mrs den Haag, and Aletta is my daughter.

No one can take her away from me.

LOUISE put her pen down and read the words out aloud. They sounded good—no, they sounded wonderful! The culmination of so many dreams. A strong supportive man as her husband and his child to love and take care of.

A little cloud passed in front of the sunshine of her happiness and cast a shadow.

'It doesn't matter,' she muttered defiantly. 'It doesn't matter one bit that they're not *really* mine—they're my second chance at having a real family.' And she drew her shoulders back into a determined line. She would make it work out. Make it work out so well that in the end no one would be able to tell that it started out as make-believe.

And maybe, if she was really lucky. . .

With a firm shake of her head she put her final dream away. That was one dream she didn't dare try to fulfil, especially now that she had so much to lose.

Her dark secret had destroyed her first chance and had nearly destroyed her. She would never take that chance again. The secret was one she had to keep.

Several days passed in relative harmony. Louise was carefully feeling her way over Jacob's likes and dislikes and coming to terms with the impossibility of

77

preparing meals for erratic mealtimes.

Granted, Jacob had quickly realised that the atmosphere at home was sweeter if he remembered to phone when he was delayed. And he was always appreciative of her efforts—even though she sometimes had the feeling that he could have done better himself. But there was still a strange feeling in the house once he came home, as if the two of them were walking round each other on tiptoe.

Two subjects seemed to bridge the chasm between them—their mutual interest in medicine and the rapidly growing bond formed by their love of Aletta.

Even so, Louise was finding her days very empty, especially after the non-stop work in SCBU, and wondered how soon it would be practicable for her to return to part-time work.

She knew from what Jacob had told her that they were still short-handed in the unit and, although not all the beds had been in use when she had spoken to him last night, that situation could change at less than a moment's notice.

Having thought of all the possibilities, Louise decided to broach the subject with Jacob.

'After dinner would be a good time,' she murmured to herself as she made preparations for Jacob's favourite dishes. 'If I get this in the oven before I feed Aletta it should all be ready when he walks in the door.'

She had been congratulating herself on Aletta's smooth transition from bottle-feeding to the breast when, at the crucial moment, the whole system was cast into disarray.

'Come on, darling. What's the matter?' she crooned as the little mite fussed and grizzled for no apparent reason. 'I wish you could tell me what's wrong.'

'*Is* something wrong?' The unexpected sound of

Jacob's voice startled her and she swung round to face him, the baby held up against her exposed breast.

'Not really.' Her surprise at seeing him standing there so tall and broad and distinguished in his charcoal-grey suit made her voice emerge as a breathless squeak.

'Has she finished feeding?' He walked towards them, his hands reaching for Aletta. 'I could bring her wind up, if you like.'

'Little monkey hasn't had *any* milk yet. I don't know why.' She turned Aletta towards her father, completely forgetting that her naked breast would be revealed until the air chilled her.

Her eyes flew to his and found them riveted on the exposed creamy flesh. They remained frozen in a startled tableau until Aletta wriggled and flailed one arm while complaining loudly.

'Has. . .' He paused to clear his throat. 'Has she had anything at all?'

'Nothing,' she confirmed. 'I can't seem to get her interested in trying.'

'Perhaps she needs to get a taste to remind her what she's missing. That sometimes happens because it's harder work for the baby to feed from the breast. They actually have to work to get the milk out, whereas with a bottle, it almost falls into their mouth and they just have to swallow.' He spoke soothingly and Louise felt her frustration easing. 'Shall I try something and see if it helps?'

'I thought I'd tried everything, but if you think you can work miracles. . .' Her tone was a disgruntled challenge.

'Let's see, shall we?' He raised one dark eyebrow and his eyes gleamed at her as he picked up the gauntlet. 'First of all,' he directed as he removed his jacket and rolled the sleeves of his immaculately white shirt to reveal the golden strength of his hair-dusted forearms, 'get Aletta comfortable on your arm and then relax your elbow so that she is almost resting on your lap.'

He helped to settle Aletta in position, taking time to stroke the fussy baby's downy cheek with the backs of his fingers.

'Right,' he continued, fixing his gaze on hers. 'Let's try a variation on a theme,' and one lean tanned hand encircled the engorged globe gently until it was cradled in the warmth of his palm.

Louise stiffened at the contact, her pulse suddenly racing.

'Uncomfortable?' he queried solicitously.

'N-no.' It was *her* voice that was husky now.

'Good. Just relax. It should be perfectly painless, or I'm not doing it right.' He gazed deeply into her eyes, his own darkly dilated as he stroked the fingers of his other hand down over the curve of her breast until they reached her nipple.

'I already tried. . .' She started to speak but the words were frozen in her throat as he let go of his hold on her nipple with his fingers and replaced the contact with his own mouth.

Shock held her immobile until she gasped aloud as he drew her nipple deeply into his mouth and suckled her. The exquisite sensation was compounded by the erotic sight of his tanned face against the smooth ivory of her breast, his mouth enclosing not just her nipple but her areola as well, his eyelashes lowered in a dark crescent on his flushed cheek.

Involuntarily, her free hand came up to smooth the errant strands from his forehead and stroke them back into position, then lingered, drawn irresistibly by the solid warmth of his skull.

He drew deeply on her breast and the strength of the resulting contraction of her uterus made her clench her hand in the pale silky strands in sweet agony.

Simultaneously she felt her milk start to flow in profusion and was stunned to see Jacob swallow. His eyes opened suddenly, the lashes sweeping upwards to allow the midnight blue of his widely dilated pupils to meet her own startled stare.

Holding her gaze for several long seconds, he again drew on her and swallowed, almost defiantly, before slowly withdrawing.

The continuing flow from her nipple left a drop of milk on the fullness of his lower lip and before she realised what she was doing, Louise had flicked the tip of her tongue over her own lip. Her eyes widened as she saw him mimic her action and collect the errant drop with the slow sweep of his tongue.

'Now,' his voice was so husky that he had to pause to clear his throat. 'Now try Aletta at your breast.' He moved back slightly.

'Aletta. . .?' Her voice was dazed with the events of the past few seconds.

'Now that the milk is flowing she might be more interested.' And he cupped his long lean fingers under the tiny head to position her.

Effortlessly Aletta opened her little mouth and started to suckle as if there had been no problem, but Louise hardly noticed. As soon as Jacob's mouth had touched her she had forgotten she was holding his child. Her whole existence had been encompassed by the reality of what he was doing to her.

'Louise. . .' Her unnatural stillness and silence had drawn his attention, her gaze fixed blindly on the baby at her breast.

'Louise, look at me. Please. . .' It was the accented entreaty in his voice which finally caught her attention, and she looked up at him.

There was a strange expression in his eyes, almost of fear, but it was swiftly hidden.

'Did it upset you? What I did to you. . .to your breast just now?' He was speaking softly so he didn't disturb the feeding child.

Upset me? she queried silently. No! Enthrall me, delight me, excite. . .

'No, Jacob,' she spoke equally softly, grateful that it hid the quiver in her voice. 'You were only doing it to help Aletta. And anyway, why should such a natural process be upsetting. . .?'

'Ah, yes. For Aletta.' He paused, his mouth pursed in thought before he straightened slowly to his full height. 'Louise. . .' He paused.

Was this Mr den Haag, consultant, being so indecisive?

'We need to have a talk. Later. After you have finished with Aletta. Is there anything I can do for the meal?'

Suddenly she remembered her plans for the evening. The plans Aletta had ruined.

'Oh, no!' she wailed softly as she glanced up at the clock, the windmill's arms telling the tale, 'I forgot to watch the time.'

'Has something been in the oven too long? I didn't smell anything when I came in.'

'No, you wouldn't because it hasn't started cooking yet! I left it all ready and it should have gone in fifteen minutes ago.'

'If I put it in straight away, will it still be all right? If not I could make something.'

'No, it will be fine, but I won't have time to have

a bath and change my clothes before it's finished.'

'But the dress you are wearing is very becoming.' His accent had strengthened as his eyes travelled over the unbuttoned front of her fine wool dress. 'Why don't you leave that one on?'

'It won't be the same.' She heard the petulance in her own voice. 'I wanted everything to be. . .' She stopped before the words could spill out, but he tried to guess, anyway.

'Is it a special occasion? Your birthday?'

'Not really. I mean, no, it's not my birthday and it's not really a special occasion but I wanted to talk to you after dinner and. . .'

'What about?' There was a hint of a gleam in his eye as he teased. 'It must be important if you wanted to dress up specially?'

Aletta finished feeding at that moment and Louise's attention was divided.

'I'm sorry. Can it wait until after dinner?'

'All right,' Jacob laughed. 'You can keep your secret until after dinner. In the meantime, what do you want me to put in the oven?'

Louise gave him his instructions and swiftly completed the ritual of settling Aletta for sleep.

'Goodnight, sweetheart. Wish me luck with your Daddy,' she whispered as she brushed a kiss on a velvety cheek.

As she came downstairs a frantic ten minutes later she heard the sound of music from the lounge and drew in a steadying breath.

Smoothing down the calf-length skirt of an amber silk dress she ran her fingers along the string of matched pearls her grandparents had given her for her twenty-first birthday. She'd had to forgo the bath but

her minimal make-up was perfect and she knew Jacob
liked this dress.

It took only a few minutes to make the necessary
adjustments to the various dishes before she straightened up from the fridge with a bottle of his favourite
wine in her hands.

'Right,' she muttered under her breath. 'I don't
know what he wanted to talk about, but if this meal
doesn't put him in a good enough mood to listen to
my plans, then nothing will.' And she drew herself up
to her full height and straightened her shoulders as if
going in to battle.

'Jacob,' she called as she carried the wine towards
the dining-room. 'Everything is ready now, if you'd
like to come. . . Oh!' He had appeared at the door of
the lounge just as she had seen what he had done in
the dining-room.

Candles gleamed over silver cutlery and the small
posy of flowers she had arranged in the unused sugar
bowl which matched his china stood in pride of place
as a centrepiece.

'Do you approve?' His voice was slightly hesitant.

'Oh, Jacob!' Looking up at him, her eyes gleamed
with golden lights in the glow of the candles. 'It looks
wonderful.' She tore her gaze away from him to survey
the special touches he had put to the room, afraid that
if she looked at him any longer she might lose control
of her tongue. Then, who knew what secrets might be
revealed?

By the time they had worked their way through a
delicate salmon dish and *boeuf en croûte* to individual
raspberry pavlovas and coffee Jacob was forced to
comment.

'Now I know I'm in big trouble.' The tone was wry.

'Trouble? What do you mean?'

'When a woman makes the effort to cook all of her husband's favourite dishes for one meal, she has definitely got something important on her mind. What is the expression? The way to a man's heart is through his stomach? Well, after a meal like that, I doubt that there is anything I could refuse you.'

The candlelight glinted on the smooth edges of his teeth and gleamed over the sculpted forehead and cheekbones. She had been aware throughout the meal that his eyes had been travelling over her; her face, her hair, the pearls revealed at the base of her throat, and it had been obvious that he liked what he saw.

Now, all she had to do was translate his satisfaction after a good meal and his approval with her appearance into approval of her plans.

Suddenly she found that her hands were trembling and she rushed into speech.

'If you'd like to go through to the other room while I finish clearing the table. . .'

'We'll clear the table together, then we'll both go through.' And he started collecting cutlery. 'Then we can have our little talk.' His voice had become deeper and his eyes gleamed down at her from between sooty lashes.

All too soon the job was done, and with Jacob brushing against her as they moved around the kitchen, she was totally unable to control the steady gallop of her heart.

With no excuses left to delay the moment, she followed him through and settled herself into the corner of the settee, surprised when, instead of sitting in his usual chair where the lamp would throw light on his book when he read in the evening, he sat down beside her and took hold of her hand.

'The scene is set,' he murmured softly. 'Now, who

is going to go first? Age before beauty, or ladies first?'

Before Louise could comment, he added cryptically, 'Perhaps it will turn out the same.'

She paused for a moment, trying to fathom his meaning, then decided to introduce her topic gently.

'How do you think Aletta has settled in? She seems quite happy, doesn't she?'

One dark eyebrow lifted a fraction and a hint of a smile touched the corners of his mouth.

'She is thriving,' he confirmed wholeheartedly. 'You are a wonderful mother to her.' He squeezed the hand he held gently.

'It isn't difficult,' Louise demurred, then saw an opening. 'She's such a good baby and she still spends a lot of her time sleeping. . .' She glanced up out of the corner of her eye to gauge his mood. 'It made me think. . . Well. . . I've got so little to do when she's asleep, and. . . You said yourself that the unit is short-staffed without me until they can——'

'No!' Effortlessly he rose from the settee to tower over her like an avenging angel. His face had changed, too. Now there was no sign of an indulgent smile.

'I will not permit it. Not this time.' She had never heard his voice so harsh.

'I beg your pardon?' Suddenly Louise wished she had not eaten so well. She felt quite sick. 'Did you say you will not "permit" it? What exactly do you mean?'

'Exactly what I say.' His expression was grim. 'We made an agreement and I insist that you stick to it. My little daughter will not be left to the tender mercies of babysitters.'

'I see.' She was keeping her voice calm, but it was an effort. 'And did our agreement specify that I was to spend twenty-four hours a day, seven days a week in her company? Are *you* not going to be spending any time with her, or does the agreement only work one way?' She was starting to warm up to her argument when he broke in.

'Her mother was going to abandon her in favour of her precious career and I swore it would not happen. . .'

'Just. . .one. . .minute. . .sir!' she hissed furiously. 'I am her mother now and *I* love her. I have never suggested—never even thought about—abandoning her to a string of babysitters. I also never thought that you would be so selfish as to expect me to stay at home whether she needs me or not.'

'What are you saying? That a baby doesn't need her mother?'

'Not when she's sound asleep, she doesn't.' Louise couldn't help sounding triumphant.

'So.' His accent was growing heavier. 'You want to take up night duty so that she is left in my care. But what will happen when I am called in for an emergency? And when will Aletta ever be a part of a real family if one of us is always at work?'

'I didn't suggest doing nights. I've always hated night duty.'

'Well, then. What *are* you suggesting?' His expression was still stony and his tone harsh.

'Is there any point in telling you? It's obvious you've already made up your mind to disagree with anything I say.'

She watched a slow tide of red creep over his cheekbones and, from the corner of her eye, saw him clench his hands tightly into fists before relaxing them with a deep sigh.

'I apologise.' He gave a slight bow before he sat himself on the settee again. 'Of course, you are right. It is hardly fair for me to expect you to have sole care

of Aletta for twenty-four hours a day. It is not as if
she is your child. . .'

He was stopped by the sound of her sharp gasp of
anguish at his seemingly casual assertion.

'And you think that because I did not give birth to
her I love her any the less?' She found it difficult to
force the words past the tightness in her throat and
shook her head against the hot press of tears behind
her eyes.

'I'm sorry.' He reached out to capture the hands
which writhed against each other in graphic illustration
of her pain. 'Please,' as she pulled against his grasp,
'you know how I lose my grasp of language when I
am too close, too involved. . . Forgive me. I did not
intend that you should think that I would believe. . .
Oh! It becomes worse!' He sighed explosively in his
exasperation.

'I will start again, if you will permit?' He pulled a
wry face. 'I am sure that you would not wish to neglect
my Aletta. . .'

'Is she not mine, too, now?' Her interruption came
in a small faint voice before she raised hopeful dark
eyes to meet the deep sapphire of his. 'I do love her,
you know. So much that I could not bear for anything
to happen to her.'

'You are right, once again. Of course she is your
daughter too. You are a wonderful mother. This is
why I can't understand why you should want to leave
her while she is so small.'

'But I don't,' she asserted eagerly. 'You know that
I would be able to take her with me and leave her in
the crèche at the hospital while I'm working. While
she is so small it would not make any difference to her.'

'I suppose you are right,' he conceded grudgingly.
'And we both know that your expertise is in short

supply. . .' His words tailed off and he shook his head slightly while he gazed at her thoughtfully.

'Does any of this have a bearing on what you wanted to talk about this evening?' Louise suddenly remembered that he had said he wanted a word with her, too.

'Only indirectly,' he murmured, then drew in a breath as if he had made a decision. 'Partly I wanted to tell you that I have been asked to stand in as a guest lecturer in Sheffield—you know they have an SCBU like ours—and to ask if you would like to come with me for the trip.' He was keeping his expression so carefully neutral that she had no idea whether he wanted her to come with him or not.

'Also,' he added nonchalantly, 'I will be going over to Holland, to my old hospital, for a slightly longer time.' He smiled briefly. 'You are invited to accompany me on that trip too.'

'Holland!' She couldn't hide the start of excitement in her voice. 'I've never been there before. When are you due to go? Will we be meeting your family there?'

He grimaced briefly and there was an infinitesimal pause before he started speaking.

'The trip north is in two days and is only an overnight stay, but the trip to Holland is the following week and will take four or five days.'

'Do you think two trips so close together might be too much travelling for Aletta? Especially if we get the chance to visit some of your old childhood haunts. Perhaps it would be better if we just went to Holland with you?'

'If you think that would be best,' he agreed calmly. 'Also, I suggest that as you will be coming away with me, we put off any decision about your return to SCBU until then?' His tone made it a question but the words made it plain that he wanted her to agree.

When she didn't answer immediately the beginnings of a frown pleated his forehead.

'Are you very unhappy, Louise? To be staying at home?'

The low-voiced query carried a touch of sadness.

'Not. . .unhappy, exactly,' her thoughts were split between divining the reason for his sadness and trying to put words to her own feelings. 'It's just. . .there isn't enough to do!'

'There speaks someone accustomed to being rushed off her feet all day!' He was only half teasing.

'Exactly!' she agreed promptly. 'And I *like* being busy. Oh, I realise that Aletta will become much more of a handful when she gets a little older, but at the moment, while she's still sleeping so much of the day. . . And, anyway, I miss my patients. . .'

'*Our* patients!'

'Yes. Our patients.' She smiled up at him in shared amusement. 'We have *them* in common too, and I appreciate you telling me how they're getting on when you come home, but it's not the same. I want to see it happening for myself. I want to help them too.'

'I understand how you feel.' One arm slid across her back and settled around her shoulders to give her a slight squeeze and she welcomed the warm feeling of companionship. 'I'm the same when I have to go away for a few days. Oh, you remember the gastroschisis who arrived out of the blue?'

'Yes. That was the day you asked me to give my milk to Aletta.' She smiled reminiscently, meeting his dark blue gaze.

'Well, he went home today, with a clean bill of health on all systems. Barring anything unforeseen, we're unlikely to see him in SCBU again.'

'That's wonderful! He was a real little fighter, wasn't he. He didn't stay long with us before he was well enough to transfer to the other ward.' She smiled, pleased with the news. 'What about my little prem? The last one I specialled?'

'I don't know.' He shook his head, concern clear on his face. 'Her bradycardia, when her heart rate slows below fifty beats a minute, has become more frequent —she sets off the bleep so often they've nicknamed her "hasty Hannah".'

'It's not a good sign, though, is it?'

'Unfortunately, no. We're giving her a drug but I've increased the frequency of clinical, laboratory and X-ray assessment.'

'You don't think it's necrosis of intestinal mucosa, when the mucus lining is dying?' the worried tone in her voice echoed the severity of the possibility.

'So far, her gut pictures seem to be clear. No signs of gangrene or perforation. She's even put on a little weight in spite of the vomiting.'

'That could be caused by the drug, couldn't it?'

'Could be. We'll just have to wait and see.'

As the conversation dwindled, Louise found her head resting against the smooth fabric covering the muscled breadth of his shoulder and breathed in the evocative hint of his shaving soap as if it were a natural everyday occurence. She stiffened slightly, wondering if he would object.

'Relax,' he murmured. 'We both need time to be together, to practise being a couple. Don't you agree?'

'Yes, I suppose we do. We weren't much more than strangers when we married. . .' She allowed her words to tail off into silence.

'Louise. . .?' Jacob's voice was soft in the quiet room but because she was leaning against him she had felt a strange tension taking hold of him.

'Mmm. . .?'

'Are you falling asleep?' She felt the soft brush of his fingers across her temple.

'No. Just too comfortable to bother moving.' She gave a lazy chuckle.

'Then, perhaps this is a good time to talk about what happened this evening?'

She started to raise her head from his shoulder but he cradled her with one broad palm and persuaded her to return.

'No. Don't move.' He stroked his hand over the soft cap of curls as if he enjoyed their texture. 'I did not mean to spoil your relaxation, but we need to talk of it.'

'Why? You were only helping Aletta. . .'

'Is that all it seemed to you? That I was only helping my daughter to feed?' Blunt disbelief filled his voice. 'You can't be that naïve!'

He had tilted her head until he could look down into her face, his own filled with a strange angry tension.

'Louise. . .' He cupped her cheeks in his palms, 'You must know that I find myself very attracted to you. That this evening, when I suckled you. . .'

She felt the fiery heat fill her cheeks at his explicit reminder of what had happened.

'Yes,' he hissed softly. 'You do well to blush so sweetly. Just so did your breast warm for me when I touched it, when I took it in my mouth. . .'

'Jacob!' She was embarrassed and confused and, worst of all, she could feel herself becoming aroused just listening to the eroticism of his words. 'We had an agreement,' she demurred. 'We only married for Aletta's sake.'

'Did we?' he countered. 'Can you truly say that you feel nothing for me? That you will be perfectly happy to live the rest of your life treating each other as brother and sister?'

Louise was taken aback by his unexpected vehemence.

'What do you mean?' Her voice was faint with sudden fear. 'Have you changed your mind about the marriage? Isn't it working out the way you wanted for Aletta?'

Why, oh, why had she mentioned the idea of going back to work. Now it seemed as if he was regretting their arrangement and she was going to lose Aletta. . . and Jacob.

'No, not for Aletta. For me,' he growled the words towards the fireplace as his cheeks darkened. 'I find that I want this to be a proper marriage.' He turned to face her again, piercing her with his eyes. 'I want you.'

'But. . .' After several stunned seconds she still couldn't get her brain working.

'You would not have to decide now, tonight.' He was looking down at his hands where they lay clenched together, his absurdly dark lashes casting long shadows over the deepened colour of his cheekbones.

Louise felt quite detached from the situation, almost as if it were happening to someone else as she let her eyes travel greedily over the perfectly sculpted symmetry of his face.

Suddenly, he looked up, his expression quite fierce.

'It would give us a chance to be a *real* family, not just halfway. Wouldn't you like that?'

'I'm sorry.' For a moment she thought she must have missed part of the conversation. 'I'm not sure what you mean. . .'

'Wouldn't you like Aletta to have some companionship?'

'You mean you would employ a nanny instead of

letting me take her into work with me?'

'No, I would prefer if that were not necessary, for Aletta's sake. Actually, I was thinking that we could perhaps decide to provide her with a little brother or sister.'

There was a long silence before Louise spoke.

'Don't you think it's a little early to think about that? She isn't quite two months old yet, and to start thinking about adopting a second child while she is so small. . .'

'I didn't mean for us to adopt.'

His words fell into a bottomless void.

At first, Louise couldn't believe what he was suggesting. Then, she couldn't bear the pain it caused.

'No!' The vehemence of her denial was unmistakable and full of the pain of denying herself a second chance to fulfil her dream.

'I apologise,' Jacob's manner was stiff. 'I hadn't realised that you found me so repellent.' And he started to get up from his seat.

'No!' Louise clutched at his sleeve and held on tightly so that he was temporarily unable to leave her. 'That's not what I meant at all,' she gabbled hastily.

'Then, what did you mean?'

Although he had remained seated beside her, he wasn't trying to look at her.

'I don't find you. . . You aren't. . .' She closed her eyes and shook her head in frustration before taking the plunge. 'I find you very attractive, both as a person and as. . .as. . .' her courage failed her.

'As attractive as I find you.' The words were softly spoken and accompanied by the gentle touch of his hand on her cheek. Her eyes opened to gaze straight up into his. 'I find you very attractive——' his voice was husky as he repeated her words '——both as a person and as the woman I want to make love with.'

The final words were spoken against her lips before he took them in a kiss of such gentle caring that she was lost before she could think to object.

For long moments he cherished her mouth with a display of such sweet passion that she forgot to breathe lest he should stop weaving his magic.

Finally, he drew away just far enough to bury his face in the softness of her slender neck, murmuring almost incoherently.

'Now we will really be able to be a family,' he muttered into the silkiness of her honey-coloured curls.

Instantly, she stiffened in his arms.

'Jacob, I can't. I daren't.' Her voice throbbed with sincerity. 'It's not because I don't want you.' She felt her face heating with embarrassment at her own brazen words.

'I see,' he said heavily. 'It's just that you don't want to have my baby.' There was desolation in his eyes before he shuttered them.

'You know that's not true. I love Aletta and if. . . if only things were different. But they aren't.' She was filled with sadness. 'I lost everything once and. . .and I couldn't bear for it to happen again.'

'Ah! It is all too recent for you to have come to terms with it all. Just you wait. Eventually you will have your courage back. Then you will remember that your chances of having another baby like your Matthew are very slim, especially with all the recent research that's been going on.' He cradled her head against his broad shoulder and rocked her as if she was a fragile child.

'There's no hurry,' he soothed. 'We've got all the time in the world to decide what we want to do. For now, we'll just continue to get to know each other until the time feels right.'

Held in his strong arms, Louise felt more secure than
at any other time in her life, and her heart swelled
with joy.

Maybe everything would turn out right after all.
Maybe lightning didn't strike twice in the same place,
but did she dare tempt fate? This time she had so much
more to lose.

# CHAPTER SIX

'I MISS him,' she confided to her diary the next night. 'Not just the presence of another person in the house, but Jacob, himself.' She stroked the top of her pen repeatedly over her lower lip as she gazed unseeingly at the elegant curtains drawn to close out the darkness.

It wasn't until he suggested having a baby that I realised how much I wanted to. Not just to have a baby, as it was with Colin, but to have *his* baby. Then I realised how much I wanted him, whether we had a baby or not. Am I falling in love with him?

'Do you think I'm falling in love with your Daddy, Aletta?' she crooned as she lifted her out of her cot. 'You love him, don't you? You've started smiling at him when he comes in the room and you recognise his voice, too, don't you, you clever girl.'

She settled herself in the nursing chair and prepared to feed her, a vivid image of Jacob's mouth at her breast flashing into her memory and speeding her pulses with a jolt.

'Perhaps I'll know when he comes back,' she mused softly, stroking Aletta's silky hair gently while she suckled. 'Perhaps I won't be able to help myself from smiling at him like you do and wanting him to pick me up and cuddle me.' She stopped. 'Good lord. What nonsense I'm talking. You'd better not tell him!'

In her heart of hearts she knew it wasn't nonsense.

She *did* want to smile when Jacob came home, she
was smiling now just thinking about it, and she would
like nothing better than to be held in his powerful arms
and cuddled—and so much more. . .

'It's not just because of the way he is with you,' she
continued her one-sided conversation with a bright-
eyed Aletta, 'although that must be part of it. He's
such a big powerful man, but he's so gentle with you.'
She leant down to brush a kiss on a downy cheek.
'You and I both know we can trust him. Trust him
not to use his strength against us, to take care of us.'

She was silent for a while as her thoughts
rambled on.

'. . .And his kisses!' The spasm which gripped her
at the thought of the sensations he had aroused in
her with those perfectly chiselled lips and that warm
tongue. . .'Good heavens! You shouldn't be listening
to this, sweetheart. It'll be years before you need to
know about the things a man's kisses can do to you.
God knows it took me enough years to find out that
kissing was a game for two to enjoy, rather than one
to inflict and the other submit to. . .'

When Jacob returned the following evening, Louise
had just settled herself down to write in her diary.

Hearing the sound of the front door closing, she
rose instantly to her feet, her heart beating urgently
in her chest.

'He's home!' she whispered to the silent room.
'Jacob's home!' and she flew out of the room, her feet
scarcely touching the deep pile of the carpet.

Reaching the top of the stairs she paused, suddenly
uncertain of Jacob's response if she was to fling herself
into his arms as she suddenly wanted to.

He had his back to her as he removed his coat and

hung it up, his suitcase and briefcase neatly side-by-side at his feet. She saw him pause and stiffen before he spun round smoothly on the balls of his feet.

Their eyes met instantly, searing sapphire-blue locking with darkly heated honey and then he was moving, taking the stairs two at a time to arrive swiftly in front of her without once breaking the visual connection between them.

For long seconds they stood at the top of the stairs with scarcely room for a breath of wind to pass between them and then she was in his arms and lifted right off her feet as their lips met in a kiss of earth-shattering intensity.

Finally they parted, totally breathless.

'Oh, Louise,' he sighed huskily, holding her tight and swinging her round in a circle. 'I missed you.' The words were uttered like a vow as his eyes impaled her. 'I don't want to go away without you again. . .' He halted suddenly as if he had not expected to hear himself say the words aloud and a tide of colour darkened his cheeks.

'I missed you too,' Louise whispered, and saw the instant reaction her words caused in the dilation of his pupils.

'Ah, *lieveling*, I hoped you would, but I didn't know if you would say it.'

'*Leave*. . .? What did you call me?'

He looked away briefly as if embarrassed before answering.

'*Lieveling*. It's Dutch. It means something like "little one".'

'It sounded strange.'

'You don't like it, that I speak Dutch words to you?' his accent had returned with a vengeance.

'No! I like it. I like your accent too. It sounds. . .'

'What?' he prompted, no doubt intrigued by the way she had suddenly stopped speaking. 'How does it sound to you?'

He had lowered her so that her feet were once more in contact with the floor. With one lean finger he tilted her chin until their eyes met.

'It sounds,' she whispered slowly as she gathered her courage, 'very sexy. . .'

'God!'

Almost before the words were out of her mouth he had swept her up in his arms and was striding towards their bedroom, his mouth covering hers with explicit fervour.

Louise was so enthralled by his kiss that she felt as if she was floating until at last he lowered her gently on to their bed, stretching out beside her to begin his exploration of her lips all over again.

'Oh, Louise. . .' he groaned against the smooth column of her throat before he leant over her, supporting his weight on his arm.

She was surrounded by him, cradled by the strength of the arm circling her body and breathing in the musky essence of his skin, his tongue starting an erotic foray into the sweet darkness of her mouth.

One hand cradled the side of her face, his thumb stroking over her cheek while he angled her head to permit ever deeper penetration, teasing and tempting her into an unseen slippery duel.

She was only hazily aware of the exploration undertaken by his other hand. All she knew was that wherever he lingered, her nerves became almost unbearably sensitised, spreading a strange tingling warmth throughout her body.

When she finally felt his touch on the naked skin of her shoulder, it was only with a sense of relief that he was at last giving her what she hadn't even known she craved.

'Jacob,' she gasped breathlessly as he released the catch on her bra and captured the breast which gleamed like a pearl in the subdued light.

'You are so beautiful,' he whispered as he paused to admire the smooth symmetry of her tautly swollen globes. He teased each nipple in turn, smiling at her as they peaked willingly for him.

'May I?' he queried softly, his tongue flicking out to moisten the tip of one. 'This time, not for Aletta but just for me.'

'Yesss. . .' It was a sublime mixture of ecstasy and agony when he finally took her in his mouth, taunting and tantalising her with a sublime array of flicks and nips and gliding strokes moving almost desperately from one to the other until at last his control broke and he suckled her deeply.

'Oh. . .! Oh, God. Please!'

Louise arched convulsively upwards, offering her breasts for his delight, only hazily conscious that her hips too had signalled her desperation for his attention.

The broad warmth of his hand cradling the moist nakedness of her feminity was the first clear realisation she had that Jacob had removed her clothing.

Through half-open eyes she saw the subdued gleam of light on the muscled breadth of his naked shoulders and felt the exquisite sensation as her hyper-sensitive nipples were abraded by the silky pelt on his chest.

A tiny warning voice fought to be heard but was buried under an avalanche of sensation as Jacob started to kiss his way from her breasts down towards the shadowy indentation of her navel.

He shifted his position slightly to allow him greater access. At the same time that Louise was suddenly made aware of the fully erect evidence of his masculinity, Jacob moved his hand to explore her intimately for the first time.

'No!'

Her voice was panic-stricken and she tried to push him away.

'I can't. . .I can't.' Her breathing sounded like tiny sobs as she braced her slender palms against him.

'Stop!' he rasped as he rolled away and reached behind him to pull one layer of covers over his hips, dislodging her diary to fall to the carpet with a thud.

'Louise, I would never force you to do something you didn't want. Do you not know that? Do you trust me so little?'

The hurt sounding so clearly in his voice stilled her frantic efforts to fasten her buttons instantly, and she made do with holding the edges together with her folded arms.

'I am a big man—I can't help that—but I am not an animal.' He closed his eyes but not soon enough. She had seen the pain he was hiding. 'I would have made certain that I did not hurt you, especially as you are so small.'

'Oh, Jacob.' She was close to tears, knowing instinctively that his reaction was to a fresh scar on his male pride. Who had hurt him so badly in the past? Aletta's mother?

'You have misunderstood,' she said simply.

'How?' He was lying on his back, now, one arm thrown across his eyes and one knee raised to hide his arousal from her. 'How have I misunderstood? You shouted, "No," and fought with me to stop me. How could I misunderstand this? It is very clear—I frighten you and you do not wish for me to make love with you. So?' he challenged.

'Oh, Jacob.' She gave in to temptation and stroked his arm, marvelling at the taut power concealed under smooth golden hair-sprinkled skin.

He tensed at her touch and she was not certain if it signalled rejection. She grasped his wrist and tried to lift his arm from his face but he resisted.

'Please, Jacob.' For the first time she used the Dutch pronunciation of his name. 'Look at me.'

She felt his arm relax then felt the sleek contraction of his muscles as he lifted his arm and let it drop on the bed above his head.

Louise felt the flush invade her cheeks as she was confronted by the vulnerability of his hair-tufted arm-pit, the tension along his ribs drawing them upwards and hollowing his belly into a dark shadow where it disappeared under the bedspread.

He had been watching her slow perusal of his body and when her eyes finally reached his, the pupils were so widely dilated that they appeared black.

'I am not, nor have I ever been, frightened of you,' she stated firmly in spite of the fact that the expression in his eyes had just doubled her heart-rate. 'I have known you, in a professional capacity, for over a year. I have seen you dealing with tiny babies and their distraught parents over and over again. I don't believe you have it in you to be cruel or hurtful.'

'Then, why?' It was a cry from the heart. 'You think I am too big? Like an animal, so you do not desire me.'

'Yes, I suppose you are like an animal. . .' She saw him tense but continued, 'A golden, powerful, big hunting cat, and dangerously beautiful.' She had put all her feelings into her words until they rang out like a paean of praise.

He was stunned into immobility, his heart pounding visibly in the depth of his chest.

'Ah, Louise.' He drew in a deep breath as if he had been underwater a very long time. 'But. . .I don't understand yet.'

One large long-fingered hand reached out to mesh tightly with hers.

'Explain,' he demanded fiercely. 'If you look at me like this, how can it be that you do not want to make love with me.'

'But I do.' She squeezed his hand tightly, feeling the blush rising in her cheeks again. 'I *do* want to make love with you, but I'm not protected.'

'Protected? Ah, yes, I understand. But Louise, it is probably not necessary. You are breast-feeding Aletta and your periods have only just returned.' For a second she was taken aback that he would know such a thing then realised that keen observation was part and parcel of his profession.

'Even so, there is a risk,' she insisted stubbornly.

He lay back for a few seconds, deep in thought, then rolled abruptly away from her to open the small drawer in the bedside cabinet and scrabble through the contents.

'Aha!' He held several small packets triumphantly aloft. 'I have solved the problem. . .' He was smiling mischievously until he saw the expression on her face.

'Before you let your imagination run away with you,' he warned solemnly, 'these have been in the drawer since before Aletta was conceived. I was totally faithful to my wife the whole of our marriage, in spite of the fact that we rarely slept together, and never in this room.

'Since her death,' he continued quietly, 'I did not want to want a woman. I believed there was no more place in my life for desire; that our arrangement would be enough for both of us.' He lifted long dark lashes to gaze straight at her.

'I was wrong,' he said simply and held out his hand, one small packet resting in the middle of his broad palm.

'We can't use those,' she objected. 'They have a shelf-life, don't they?'

His laughter filled the room. 'How many years do you think they have been in that drawer? Certainly not long enough to have perished!'

'I'm sorry, Jacob, but I can't. I daren't take the risk that I would have another baby like Matthew.'

She realised as soon as she said them that her words could be ambiguous, but dared not correct herself. If she did, she might have to explain too many things which were best left hidden.

'You would rather we waited until you have had time to go to the Family Planning Clinic?' he queried gently.

'Yes, please, Jacob,' she confirmed, then continued hesitantly, 'I'm sorry that I let everything get out of hand earlier on. . .'

His swift chuckle lightened the load of guilt she was carrying. 'I think we were both equally to blame for that little episode. Neither of us realised that we would burst into flames like that until it was nearly too late. At least we know now——' he fixed her with a positively lethal stare '—and we can start looking forward to it.'

His two hands came up to capture her face and he ran the tip of his tongue across his lower lip before leaning inexorably towards her.

'In the meantime,' he breathed huskily as his eyes flickered over her face and down to the shadowed cleavage revealed in the unfastened front opening of her silky dress, 'weren't we supposed to be getting to

know each other? I could show you several very enjoy-
able methods, none of which involves the slightest
chance of pregnancy!'

She had been looking up at him, mesmerised by the
expression on his face. At the last moment, just as his
head swooped down, she tilted her own head back at
an angle and parted her mouth to welcome his with
an open fervour that nearly stopped both their
hearts.

The next few days passed in a blur. Jacob had been
rushed off his feet by a series of urgent admissions and
consultations as well as by a mountain of essential
paperwork which had to be cleared before his departure for Holland.

In spite of that, Louise felt happier than ever before.

Jacob had promised to take serious note of how well
Aletta coped with her change in routine before they
made their final decision about Louise's possible return
to work—and this time it *was* going to be a joint
decision!

There was also the recent change in their relationship
to fill her mind and her heart.

Soon she would have nearly everything she had
always longed for—a home and family of her own to
love and care for and a beautiful baby to help to bring
up. When Matthew died, she had believed that she
had lost her only chance at happiness. Now. . .she had
a husband she loved and desired and who desired her
equally passionately.

She told herself that it didn't really matter that he
didn't love her—he had sworn that he would be faithful
and who knew? Perhaps one day he could grow to
love her.

In the meantime, no matter how late he returned

home or how early he had to leave for the hospital in the morning, he made a point of holding her close and kissing her with a passion which seemed to grow hotter day by day.

She had attended the Family Planning Clinic which was run at St Augustine's and had then taken the opportunity to sneak up to SCBU to visit.

She had only been there for a few minutes when Jacob arrived.

'Which one of you let him know I was here?' she accused, looking around the circle of friends and colleagues admiring Aletta.

'They didn't have to.' Jacob smiled wryly. 'I knew you wouldn't be able to resist the temptation to check up on everyone for yourself.' And he waited patiently while she peered through windows at her former charges and heard all about their progress.

'Jacob told me that the little boy with gastroschisis has gone home. What about the little prem boy—was he called Luke?'

'Lewis?' Jenny Wilson suggested.

'That's it. How's he doing?'

'He came off oxygen—in fact I'm surprised Mr—your husband didn't tell you. It caused a bit of a panic because he pulled the tube out himself and then refused to let us put it back in. We all waited for the monitor to tell us the worst but he kept breathing by himself. Quite the hero of the hour.'

'So he's moved across to the other ward?'

'Yes, and coming on by leaps and bounds.'

'What about "hasty Hannah", Carol? You took over specialling her, didn't you? How's she doing?'

'He told you about her nickname!' Carol Long laughed briefly then sobered. 'She seems to be holding her own at the moment in spite of the bradycardia.

It's not a steady gain, but she has topped the two-kilo mark for the first time.'

'You really love the work in SCBU, don't you?' Jacob commented quietly as he drove Louise and a soundly sleeping Aletta home.

Louise agreed equally quietly and the rest of the journey was filled with enough discussion of Jacob's patients and their various problems to make her feel almost as if she was once more working with him.

When he finally dropped her back home, Jacob had asked how she had got on at the Family Planning Clinic and she had detailed her progress.

'I told them that I wanted to continue feeding Aletta, especially as we're going to Holland. . .'

'You make it sound as if it's a desperately foreign country that might threaten her life in some way,' he laughed.

'Well, I thought it was important for several reasons,' she defended herself. 'Firstly, there's her allergy problem; then there's the fact that it's her routine—I wouldn't want to make any drastic changes just before we go away; then there's the fact that I *like* feeding her myself. I find it very satisfying. . .'

'All right, all right, I surrender!' He put both hands up in front of him.

'. . .And that's before I start talking about the problems involved with trying to sterilise bottles while travelling and. . .'

He silenced her very effectively by kissing her soundly.

'So,' he growled huskily several long breathless seconds later. 'What method did you decide on?'

'They suggested I take a progesterone-only pill as it won't reduce my milk production and advised me that

I must take it at the same time every day for maximum protection.' She swallowed audibly and added the final scrap of information. 'It takes forty-eight hours to reach the correct level in the body. . .'

'And are you happy with that?' He caught one of her hands and held it between both of his. 'Or would you be happier waiting longer?'

Stung by his apparent lack of eagerness, she pulled her hand away, speaking before thinking things through.

'If you prefer to wait longer, we could leave it another week, or a month or. . .'

One finger rested on her lips.

'Yesterday wouldn't be soon enough for me, but I was concerned that you might not trust the pills entirely if you had only taken three. Now, no more nonsense. Have you taken the first one already?'

'No. I thought it would make it easier to remember if I took it at bedtime.'

His eyes gleamed wickedly.

'What a good idea! Then I can remind you each night as we get into bed together!' And his lips touched hers as lightly as the drift of petals.

'Just two more nights,' he promised huskily, 'and then I shall make sure you will have the wedding-night you deserve!' This time his kiss lingered, deliciously.

'We'll have to remember to set the alarm before we go to bed or we'll never wake in time for our flight to Holland.'

That evening Louise had again been writing in her diary when Jacob returned home from an exhausting session as the whole SCBU team tried to stabilise a Down's Syndrome baby after complex open-heart surgery.

He had told her about the case before he left for the hospital that morning, concerned, as ever, about the child's chances of survival.

Apparently they had been preparing to place a valved conduit between the right ventricle and the pulmonary artery to correct a complex transposition of the great arteries.

As she heard his key in the lock at least an hour later than expected, she hoped that he hadn't been delayed by anything serious.

As she always tried to do these days, she left what she was doing to greet him with a kiss and take part vicariously in the events of the unit by listening while he told her of the day's successes and failures.

'I'm sorry to be so late.' He wrapped her in the warmth of his strong arms and kissed her lingeringly. 'You did get my message?'

'Yes. Your indispensable Mrs Moorcroft let me know.'

She was about to tighten her arms around him for a second kiss when she heard his stomach rumble.

'Come through to the kitchen and talk to me while I serve out your meal.' She linked her arm through his as they walked down the hallway. 'How did your little Down's boy cope today?'

'The Rastelli procedure went like a dream.' He sat down heavily on the corner of the kitchen table and rubbed both hands tiredly over his face. 'The problems didn't come until post-op.' He paused as she shooed him off the table and into a chair and put a steaming plate of braised steak in front of him.

He captured her hand and placed a kiss in her palm, closing her fingers over it and giving her small fist a squeeze. 'Thanks.' He looked up at her, a tired smile on his face. 'I'm more than ready for this,' and he tucked in willingly for several silent minutes.

Finally, he continued.

'For some reason, God knows why, he took a long time to stabilise after the anaesthetic wore off.'

He shrugged.

'And, of course, you stayed in the unit until the surgeon and anaesthetist were both happy with his condition,' she added wryly.

'Well. . .'

'Jacob, that wasn't a criticism. I'm just as guilty as you are when it comes to worrying about patients.'

She stood behind him and stroked both hands over his shoulders. 'And,' she added quietly, 'I bet you told whoever's specialling him that you're perfectly willing to return to the unit in the night if the child doesn't maintain his progress.'

Jacob was silent but she could see the increased colour on the back of his neck.

She patted his shoulders sharply.

'There you are! I knew you were every bit as soft-hearted as I thought.' And she leant forward to place a kiss among the thick silky strands of his silvery hair.

Jacob had a pile of paperwork to go through, so she left him to it while she had a bath and fed Aletta.

She had settled her for the night and entered their room to hear Jacob at the medicine cabinet in the bathroom.

Minutes later he emerged carrying half a glass of water.

'Open wide,' he teased, the small white pill looking positively minute between his fingers.

She smiled and obediently opened her mouth, following the tablet with an unnecessary swallow of water just to show her pleasure at his attentiveness.

She was touched that he should have thought of

bringing her pill through to her and was filled with relief that he seemed to have accepted her fear of becoming pregnant.

'Only two more days,' he growled in her ear as he pulled her into the curve of his body as she climbed into bed with him. 'I hope you manage to find some asbestos sheets soon because I think we'll both be candidates for spontaneous combustion by then.'

'You wouldn't be feeling so frustrated if you stayed on your own side of the bed,' she stated primly.

'Really?' He pretended amazement. 'And who was it who travelled all the way across to my side in the middle of the night last night? Who was it who wrapped herself around me so tightly I nearly had to remove my skin to get out of bed?'

This was a side of Jacob that had only recently started appearing. A younger, more carefree Jacob who had taken total possession of her heart.

The forty-eight hours dragged by interminably, the final straw coming less than an hour before she was expecting him home.

'Louise? It's Jacob.' It was funny that she had never noticed before that his accent was more marked on the telephone, and she smiled to herself just to hear his voice. 'I'm going to be late this evening. Probably three or four hours.'

'Oh.'

Her heart had sunk all the way to the floor.

'Yes. Oh.' His voice had dropped several tones and to half the volume. 'Don't start without me!'

'Don't. . .? Oh, Jacob, you are an idiot!'

'At least it made you smile. I'll be home as soon as I can. . .I promise!'

Aletta had been slightly fractious that evening. Whether it was because she sensed something in the air, it was difficult to tell, but it was some while before she had wanted to settle.

Louise had managed to pacify her and still managed to complete the major part of the packing for their departure in the morning. All that was left to put in now was their wash-kits and her make-up bag.

She was sitting at the dressing table having brushed her hair for the tenth time when she decided to add a few extra lines to the entry in her diary.

It's getting very late, now, and we can't afford to oversleep in the morning. By the time he gets home he'll probably be too tired to. . .

'You must be joking!' said a husky voice in her ear as he read the words over her shoulder. 'I'd have to be dead and buried to miss out on tonight.'

'Oh! Jacob, you scared me. I didn't hear you come in.' She pressed one hand to her galloping heart and leant back against him to look up at his face.

'Come on, woman. Put down that pen and come and give me my "welcome home" kiss.'

She turned round on the vanity stool, swinging her legs around the side. Before she could stand he had knelt swiftly in front of her and drawn her into his embrace, his mouth finding hers with unerring accuracy.

# CHAPTER SEVEN

AFTER looking forward to this night for so long, Louise was horrified to find herself tensing up, a quivering sensation filling her deep inside.

'Hey!' Jacob's voice was gentle as he raised her chin. 'What's this all about? Last-minute nerves?'

Louise was shocked into meeting his eyes, finding them full of understanding.

'I'm sorry,' she quavered. 'It's so stupid, I know. . .'

'Who are you calling stupid,' he countered, holding one of his own hands out in front of him to demonstrate a visible tremor.

'Jacob! But. . .'

'And you thought someone my size and age wouldn't get nervous,' he mocked himself.

Suddenly, her fears seemed too ridiculous for words and she threw her arms around him, burying her face in the hollow at the side of his neck.

'Oh, Jacob, thank you,' she murmured into his shoulder.

'What are you thanking me for? I haven't done anything yet!' he teased, and she lifted her head in time to see him waggle one eyebrow and grin infectiously. 'Now, woman,' he patted her bottom gently, 'let me get to the bathroom for a cold shower.'

'Don't you dare! You're not coming in the bed with cold feet.'

'Oh, don't worry about that. I don't think either of us is going to suffer from cold feet now.'

As she heard the sound of the shower, Louise

114

chuckled and took her robe off to drape it over the vanity stool.

She stood in front of the mirror for a moment and blinked when she saw how transparent the fine écru silk of her matching nightdress became with the light from the bedside lights behind it.

For a moment she contemplated staying exactly where she was so that Jacob would have the same view when he emerged from the bathroom, but her nerve failed her and she whirled round and sped under the covers.

'At least I now know that I've got my figure back after carrying Matthew—with a few improvements!' she murmured to herself as she looked down at a bust-line fit to flaunt. 'I wonder if I can persuade Aletta to breast-feed for the next twenty years.'

'What are you muttering about?'

She hadn't heard the water stop so she'd had no warning that Jacob was about to appear, wrapped only in a brief navy towel and carrying the ritual half-glass of water.

As he walked towards her she could see the gleam of random droplets of water left trapped in the silky pelt on his chest and her fingers itched to trace their path. Downward, through that inverted triangle and over the tautness of his belly to where the triangle broadened out again under the towel.

'If you keep looking at me like that I'm going to explode before I reach the bed,' he growled. 'Now, open wide. . .' And he touched his fingers to her lips.

This time she needed the water to swallow down the tiny tablet as her mouth was totally dry, and the oscillation of the surface of the water demonstrated the fine tremor in her hand.

'Louise. . .' Jacob stepped back from the bed and

straightened to his full height. 'Are you shaking because it is too soon. . .' His fists were clenching and releasing beside his thighs, drawing her attention to his solitary covering.

She held out one hand, palm upward, and beckoned him to move closer then patted the bed beside her.

He sat down, the overlap of the towel parting to reveal a broad wedge of muscular thigh, his weight on the side of the mattress tipping her towards him.

'I admit I'm nervous,' she said in a husky tone, 'but not because I don't want this. Perhaps it's because I've only slept with Colin before this and I don't know if I'll be able to. . .' She blushed and stumbled to a halt.

'Able to what?' he seemed a little mystified for a moment then asked. 'Was Colin a small man? Are you afraid I will squash you or. . .or tear you?'

Louise gasped as she understood what he was thinking and her cheeks became incandescent with heat.

'No! It's nothing like that. It's. . .I'm not very. . . experienced. We were only married for six weeks when we found I was pregnant and Colin never wanted to. . .I'm afraid I won't be able to. . .to satisfy you.'

'Ah, Louise. I promise that will not be a problem,' and one arm tightened around her to fit her head into the smooth curve of his shoulder.

The clean scent of the soap he had just used surrounded her and mingled with the musky undertone she had come to know as his own.

One hand stroked gently over the silky halo of curls.

'Such pretty hair,' he murmured, and she felt the kiss he pressed on to it. 'So soft and fine. It makes me think of angels.' He cupped the back of her head and tilted her face up to meet his.

'You look so dainty and fragile,' he whispered,

smoothing the curls at her temple and tracing the outline of her ear and down the slender column of her
ivory throat. 'Almost as if you would shatter if I was
too rough. . .' And he angled his head to touch her
lips in the sweetest of initiations.

After the frantic passion which had exploded
between them just the other day, this honeyed gentle-
ness was a revelation.

Louise drew in a deep, shuddering breath and
released it luxuriously as Jacob smoothed his hands
over the softly perfumed skin of her shoulders. He
rotated his palms so that the friction of the silky fabric
only increased the pleasure of his touch.

'May I. . .?' His fingers were at the first of the row
of tiny buttons which held the gown together, the softly
scooped neckline revealing the swelling glory of her
unaccustomed fullness.

'Yes. . .please!' And her own hand came up to
help him.

'No,' Jacob murmured against her palm as he kissed
it. 'I want to undress you myself. . .' His eyes were
nearly navy blue as they watched the unfastened gown
slide off her shoulders to catch briefly on the tumescent
peaks of her breasts before pooling around her waist.

He studied her for a long moment, his eyes travelling
over every softly perfumed inch before he closed his
eyes and achingly slowly lowered his head.

The touch of his lips on hers was as subtle as moon-
light. Hot and languid, it moved over hers, tasting,
exploring, promising.

His hand tangled in the silky halo of her hair and
urged her closer. She went willingly, her dusky nipples
hardening at the rough contact with his furry pelt. She
gasped and arched towards him, wanting him more
now than she had ever wanted anything in her life.

'I want to make tonight last forever,' he murmured as he traced a line of kisses along her collarbone. His hands trailed down her sides, outlining every curve until they reached the swath of silk.

'Such a tiny waist,' he marvelled as he stripped her gown away and left it to fall where it would. 'I can nearly span it with my two hands,' and he lifted her just high enough to bring her breasts up to his avidly seeking mouth.

'Jacob. . .' she moaned, spearing her fingers through the thickness of his hair and holding tight to the warm curve of the back of his skull.

Soon, that wasn't enough, and she smoothed her palms down the taut column of his neck and out to the broad strength of his shoulders. The muscles were rigid to her exploring fingertips, overlaid with smooth satiny skin. . .

Louise drew her fingernails lightly over him and he groaned, the sound seeming to come from deep in his chest, his teeth tightening reflexively on her nipple to draw an answering moan from her own throat.

Her head dropped back, exposing the long line of her neck to his pleasuring, the pulse at the base of her throat throbbing visibly.

Slowly, with absolute control, he lowered her towards the bed, the friction between their bodies a sublime torture.

'Oh. . .!' Louise stiffened slightly at her first contact with the evidence of Jacob's arousal and her simultaneous realisation that he was now as naked as she was.

Jacob raised his eyes from their preoccupation with her creamy perfection and searched her face carefully.

'I will be gentle with you. You will see. . .' He turned her slightly in his arms so that they lay side by side on the softness of fine cotton sheets.

He explored her body without hesitation, taking delight in encompassing her breasts in his broad palms and stroking his way down her side and over the curve of her hip.

She couldn't resist.

For the first time she wanted to explore, too. The firm contours of his chest felt wonderful, the silky pelt between his own sharply erect nipples tantalising the skin of her palms and enticing her to follow its path down and down. . .

'Jacob. . .!' Her breathless exclamation of his name drew his head up sharply.

'Is something wrong?' his tone was as wary as his expression.

'Oh, no, Jacob, there's nothing wrong at all. In fact you're. . .you're magnificent!'

She dragged her eyes away from her contemplation of his body in time to watch an endearing tide of colour flood upwards.

'Oh, *Jacob*,' she murmured huskily. Her hands came up to cup his fiery cheeks as she was flooded with the realisation that she loved this wonderful, vulnerable man with all her heart.

He stilled.

'Why did you call me that?' He seemed suddenly very tense.

'What?' Louise was genuinely puzzled, her thoughts filled with the revelation of her love. 'What did I say?'

'You called me Jacob,' He gave his name the continental pronunciation.

'Did I?' She paused then spoke softly, almost experimentally 'Jacob.' She smiled. 'It fits!'

'What do you mean, it fits?' Now he was confused.

'When we're here, like this,' she indicated the bed and their nakedness, 'you're Jacob. It suits you like that.' She paused again while he considered her words then added in a whisper, 'I think it sounds very sexy. . .'

She got no further.

'Louise. . .' His voice was agonised as he curled both arms around her and pulled her tightly against the length of his body, rolling over so that he lay on his back diagonally across the bed.

Louise stiffened at the unaccustomed position. She had never. . .

'Relax,' he soothed, his deep voice stroking her nerves as surely as his hands were travelling the contours of her back. 'This way I will not squash you. . .'

'But——' she interrupted, knowing he was far too sensitive about his size. She wanted to tell him that she was not worried about it but he continued speaking.

'. . .and I get the chance to touch you all over and watch you at the same time!'

His grin was pure seduction and she succumbed instantly, her bones seeming to melt away so that she was draped over him as if she had been poured.

From that moment she was his to command. Never had she realised that her body was capable of such pleasure, as he aroused her in countless different ways, encouraging her to explore for the first time the full extent of her womanhood.

Finally, even he reached the limits of his endurance.

'Louise. . .?' His hand was trembling minutely as he cupped her femininity, testing her readiness before he parted her thighs until they rested either side of his hips.

'Jacob? What. . .?'

'Shh. . . Just relax and you will see. . .' He stroked

her intimately once, twice and Louise moaned, her hips arching helplessly towards him.

'You see?' he murmured huskily, his voice heavy with arousal. 'As easy as that.' And as he thrust his hips upwards a fraction, she realised that her own convulsive movement had impaled her on his manhood.

She stilled, shocked by the fact that it had been so easy, then moved slightly, testing the sensation. . . then moved again.

'Oh, *Jacob*,' she sighed and rested her head on the breadth of his chest while she held him tight. 'Thank you.'

'Thank you? For what?' Two large hands came up to cradle her head and lift it so that he could see her face, and found her eyes full of tears.

He froze.

'Louise? What is wrong? I have hurt you?' his hands grasped her hips and he started to lift her, the muscles in his arms and shoulders tense.

'No, Jacob.' She tilted her hips instinctively to prevent his withdrawal and moaned with arousal at the increased stimulation. 'Far from it,' she gasped breathlessly. 'In fact this is the first time in my life that it hasn't hurt. . .' And she moved again helplessly.

'Ah, Louise.' He groaned and slowly started to move with her, matching his rhythm carefully to hers until her world disappeared in a dark roaring frenzy, her only reality the control he had over both of them.

'Jacob,' she sobbed aloud as she exploded into infinity and heard his own impassioned shout echo around the shadowy room mere seconds later.

'*Ik houd van jou*!'

'Was that Dutch?' she queried later as she lay draped bonelessly across him while the world slowly came back into some sort of focus.

'What?' A slight frown touched his forehead but his eyes remained resolutely closed.

'You shouted something, when you. . .' She felt her face heat. 'At the end.'

He chuckled at her evasion.

'Probably. What did it sound like?' He peered at her from under one lazy set of lashes.

'Something like *hoven*. . . I don't remember exactly. I was rather preoccupied at the time. . .'

'So I should think.' He slid both hands indolently down over her back to cup the pert globes of her buttocks and squeeze gently.

'So, what did it mean. . .?' She was quickly losing interest in the conversation as she became aware of his rapidly reviving powers.

'Just words of. . .of praise,' he murmured distractedly as his hands travelled further down the backs of her thighs, stroking the silky skin before once more urging them to part for him.

'Jacob,' she moaned mindlessly as the excitement grew, her mind hardly functioning now. 'It sounded lovely. . .' She relaxed the muscles of her pelvic floor and then tightened them against his intrusion, briefly teasing before relenting. 'Ahh. . . Yesss. . .' she hissed ecstatically. 'I shall have to. . .start. . .learning Dutch. . .' And they were the last intelligible words she spoke.

The journey to Holland went smoothly. Aletta travelled beautifully, sleeping most of the way so that Louise was able to relax and enjoy the journey.

'I'm sorry,' Jacob had apologised soon after they were settled in their seats, 'but I have some paperwork to go over before we arrive.' He had paused briefly

to grin wickedly down at her. 'I should have looked
at it last night, but I was somewhat distracted. . .'
He chuckled intimately when her cheeks grew pinker
and leant forward to leave a fleeting kiss on her
startled lips.

Her heart leapt into her throat at his apparently
casual intimacy.

'Jacob!' she admonished. 'Behave yourself!'

'Sorry!' he apologised contritely, but the brilliance
of his sapphire eyes made the word a lie.

'Oh, Jacob! What have you done to me?' Louise
wrote in her diary, then broke off to gaze out of the
window beside her, her memory replaying the scenes
of sensuous abandon which she had enacted last night.

> I never knew I could feel like this, could feel so
> deeply. He seems to deliberately make me lose all
> control while he stays. . .not calm but. . .'

She shook her head in confusion, remembering his
total dominance of their lovemaking, of himself. She
had been helpless to do anything but submit, to him
and to the power of her own feelings. Jacob had
revelled in her caresses, encouraging her to explore
and experiment but, even at the height of his ecstasy,
he had been careful not to overwhelm her; he had
never totally relinquished control.

Perhaps that's the difference between being in love
and just feeling desire, she mused. Perhaps, one day,
he'll. . .

The plane had landed and they were whisked efficiently
across the city and out to the suburbs where the
Children's Hospital and orphanage were situated.

The flat they were to occupy was in a purpose-built

block where parents and family of the sick children could stay.

Louise was surprised to be greeted in fluent English by a young woman. Jacob had obviously been telling the truth about the Dutch affinity for languages.

'The professor has asked me to be here to take care of the baby, *mevrouw*,' she announced proudly, holding out her hands for the warmly wrapped bundle.

'But. . .' Louise tightened her grasp protectively and began to protest.

'Corrie has had a great deal of practice with little ones, Louise,' he advised calmly. 'She will take care of changing Aletta while you take yourself off to the bathroom to tidy up.' He effortlessly removed Aletta from her arms and handed her over to the smiling young woman.

'Then, as soon as you've fed her, we're expected over in the hospital.'

'We. . .?'

'Of course we,' he confirmed his statement blandly. 'It is a working lunch followed by special rounds.'

'But you. . . I. . .' She shook her head. 'Why must *I* come? Won't I be in the way?'

'Certainly not.' He smiled, directing her towards a compact modern bathroom with a large shower enclosure. 'In fact you will probably turn out to be the star of the show.'

'What?' Her feet stuck to the carpet. 'What on earth do you mean?'

'You have a similar rarity value over here as you do in England. SCBUs are on the increase but there still aren't very many staff as highly qualified as you are in the field.' There was a hint of pride in his expression. 'You'll probably find that you'll get on very well with the staff here and spend hours picking each other's brains for variations in technique.'

Louise was stunned. She had thought that Jacob had invited her to come with him to Holland for company. She hadn't realised that he had intended for her to take part.

Suddenly her pulse was racing. Did this mean that he was seriously considering her return to work?

She knew that he appreciated her expertise but she had honestly believed that he would adamantly refuse to allow her to 'abandon' Aletta to someone else's care. After his furious denunciation of his wife's obsession with her career it had been almost a foregone conclusion.

Had he changed his mind; and if so, what had changed it?

In no time at all she had washed and changed out of her travel-creased clothes, donning a smartly tailored dress and jacket in a dark almond-green linen.

Jacob was waiting for her when she came out of the bathroom, Aletta settled comfortably in the crook of one arm. Louise smiled at the picture they made, his large dark-suited frame seeming massive by comparison with his tiny daughter.

'Corrie will be back in half an hour to keep an eye on her,' Jacob commented as he settled her on to Louise's lap. 'Would you like some fruit juice while you're feeding her?' he continued as he walked across to a neat little kitchenette in the corner of the room. 'The air in planes always seems to make me very thirsty.'

At her murmured assent he returned with two tall glasses clinking with ice and turned a dining chair round to straddle it, resting his arms along the back with one glass in each hand.

Louise looked up at him, reaching her free hand

out for the glass, and found him watching Aletta suckle.

As ever, his face had softened as he watched her, and when Louise took her drink from him he reached out to stroke the soft silver-blond down which covered her head.

'We see it every day in our work,' he mused quietly, 'the fantastic powers of the human body to fight to survive, even against impossible odds. . .' His words trailed into silence but his thoughts obviously continued, as did Louise's.

'Who would have believed the difference that two months would make to Aletta? When I look back to the first time I saw her. . .' Louise shook her head disbelievingly.

'Ah, but she had special help. Something that often seems to tip the balance when everything seems hopeless.' Jacob's voice was strangely husky and his tone drew her eyes up to meet his. 'She had someone who cared enough for her to spend hours talking to her, feeding her, taking care of her; someone who showed her that she was loved, that it mattered whether she lived.'

The hand which had been stroking Aletta's head came up to cup her own cheek.

'Thank you for loving my daughter. Thank you for her life.' His thumb caressed the slight flush which darkened the pale olive of the skin across her cheekbones and trailed down to pause at the corner of her mouth.

His eyes had followed the path of his wandering thumb, the strangely dark lashes flickering over the deep sapphire-blue as he watched the changing expressions on her face. Finally, as he drew the pad of his thumb over the curve of her lower lip, his eyes met hers, the irises widely dilated until they seemed almost black.

Reflexively, Louise flicked the tip of her tongue out to moisten her dry lips and found his thumb instead, the slightly salty taste exploding on her tastebuds like an exotic spice.

The sound of a sharply indrawn breath hung in the near silence of the room and it could have come from either of them—or both. Their eyes had meshed and Louise knew that she was powerless to look away even though she was sure that her heart must be in them.

To Louise's disappointment, Aletta broke the spell when she came up for air, one flailing fist narrowly missing the forgotten glass still clenched tightly in Louise's hand.

Jacob shot back the cuff of his immaculate white shirt to glance at the slim gold band of his watch then grimaced.

'Shall I bring her wind up?' he offered. His voice sounded strange until he cleared his throat, then he continued in a deeply husky tone. 'Corrie will be back in a few minutes or I would be kissing you now. And I wouldn't be stopping at kisses. . .'

He broke off as a knock sounded at the door.

He stood up and returned the chair to its rightful position before leaning down beside Louise to feather a gentle kiss over Aletta's silky head, then paused, waiting until Louise looked up at him before kissing her too.

This was no gentle feathering, though. This was a powerful open-mouthed kiss, a duel of heat and fire which took them both by storm, speeding their heartbeats to an unsteady gallop and leaving them breathless when the knock sounded again and drew them apart.

'Tonight,' he whispered gruffly, bending once more

for a fleeting touch of the tip of his tongue across the
dark lushness of her lower lip. 'Tonight,' he repeated
before he went to open the door, and it was both a
vow and a promise.

Louise had been quite taken aback by the warmth of
her welcome at lunch.

She had been prepared to find herself relegated to
second-class citizen in such august company and was
pleasantly surprised to find her opinion avidly sought
on several issues.

At first she had wondered if it was her relationship
with Jacob which had earned her acceptance, but she
soon found that, as he had suggested, it was her own
expertise in the daily battleground in an SCBU which
was the attraction.

The visit to the unit after lunch went on for much
longer than planned. Louise had been invited into the
unit and was taken from one tiny patient to another
while her opposite numbers explained the treatment
each was receiving and the purpose of any unfamiliar
equipment.

They, too, had a 'hasty Hannah', in this case a frail-
looking little boy who set off his alarms twice in the
time she was there with periods of bradycardia.

'It is such a shame,' Zuster Beckers said sadly. 'He
was doing well and his parents were just starting to
hope that he might survive. Then, this.' She shook her
neatly styled grey-blond head. 'Now they find some
shadows on X-rays of colon and ileum. Maybe it is
start of necrosis of intestinal mucosa.'

'Will they be doing an exploratory operation?'
Louise enquired, her thoughts winging back to Hannah
at St Augustine's.

'He was scheduled for tomorrow. They hope that

damaged sections could be removed, but now, with bradycardia so much worse, we wait until morning with fingers crossed.' She paused, thoughtfully before continuing. 'I may ask you something?'

'Of course.' Louise smiled.

'In your hospital, NEC is also more often happening in your unit?'

'Unfortunately, yes. And so far we can't find out why.'

'Nor do we. The only thing we find is that babies who have mother's milk almost never have this.'

The conversation continued with one of the younger nurses commenting on the problems of stopping oral feedings while maintaining hydration, but Louise's concentration had been broken.

She glanced at her watch. The discussion of breast-feeding had triggered the let-down reflex and she had only then realised that it was time to feed Aletta.

'Tomorrow is symposium of neo-natal drug addiction,' Zuster Beckers commented. 'You will come to lecture hall, too.'

'I don't know.' Louise hesitated to agree, not knowing what Jacob had arranged but wanting to attend. She was aware that this area of Holland in particular had a huge drugs problem.

'Ah, the baby,' the kindly woman supplied her own reason for Louise's equivocation. 'The feeding time must come first when they are still so small.' She glanced down at the watch pinned to the front of her uniform. 'I will take you now over to your little one before you will burst and then I shall walk across to the orphanage with you,' she said decisively, ushering Louise towards her office where she reclaimed her jacket.

'Really, there's no need for you to come with me,'

Louise demurred. 'If you show me which way. . .'

'No, no. I insist.' She smiled broadly. 'It is always a special occasion when your husband is at the orphanage for their tea.' And she set off down the corridor at a fast clip.

Zuster Beckers busied herself with making a pot of tea for the two of them, chattering all the while Aletta fed.

'You must call me Anna,' she insisted firmly. 'It will be right for us when you will come here often in the future.'

'Louise,' she reciprocated bemusedly. 'But, why will I be coming here often?'

'For the orphanage,' came the cryptic reply.

'The orphanage. . .?'

'When he visits.'

Louise shook her head. She was getting more confused by the minute.

'Who?' she demanded. 'When who visits where?'

'But, has he not told you of the orphanage?' Anna Beckers muttered furiously in unintelligible Dutch. 'Your husband is a benefactor. . .I have the right word I think. . .a benefactor of the orphanage. He visits here often so the children look forward to him. He comes now for many years.'

'Have you known him long?' Louise enquired, trying to appear nonchalant.

'Yes. A long time.'

'How did you meet? At the hospital?' Perhaps, she found herself thinking wistfully, if she could set this friendly woman chatting, she would finally learn something about her painfully reticent husband.

'No. Many years before that. Before he became as he is today. At the orphanage.'

It was so frustrating that Louise could have

screamed. Zuster Beckers was speaking in the kind of shorthand which two people used when they were both talking about a common subject. It was obvious that she knew Jacob well and believed that he had told Louise all about his childhood. In actual fact, several months after they had first become acquainted, Louise knew very little more about him than before.

'Shall I put Aletta in her cot while you get your coat?' she prompted, clearly keen to hold the child who had been smiling sweetly up at her ever since she had finished feeding. 'Corrie will be here any minute.'

Louise shrugged her shoulders as she ran a brush through her halo of pale honey curls and touched up her lipstick.

One of these days someone will tell me what's going on around here, she muttered to herself. Everyone's telling me things about Jacob and talking as if I ought to know all about it, but it might as well be Double Dutch for all I understand. She chuckled as she realised what she had said.

Their arrival at the orphanage was a revelation.

The bright and airy modern building was set in a well-equipped garden and surrounded by a cleverly childproof fence to separate it from the hospital grounds.

Inside, the noise-level was fantastic—a cacophony of shouts and screams seeming to emanate from an open door at the other end of the main corridor.

'Ah! It has started already!' Anna Beckers laughed delightedly as she hurried Louise towards the din.

She stood in the doorway of a large playroom, unable to believe what she was seeing.

More than a dozen children were milling around, some apparently desperate to escape from something fearful, while the others were attacking the unknown danger with an arsenal of multi-coloured cushions.

A deep roaring sound exploded from a pile of bodies, followed by the eruption of a large familiar body clutching a child under each arm.

Jacob stood in front of her, his hair standing out in all directions, his tie missing and his shirt hanging out over his trousers. His face was covered in an enormous grin as his two 'victims' squealed with delight.

'Having fun?'

Louise couldn't help but smile back at him, breaking into a laugh when she saw the colour touch his face.

'*Mij alstublieft.*' One little lad clutched a handful of trouser leg and looked up at him pleadingly.

'They all love him,' Anna confided to Louise while Jacob tried to show the wisdom of Solomon in exchanging two victims under his arms for one held up by his heels until honour was satisfied. 'He seems to know just how to reach them. Without his dedication. . .'

'You're not telling her all my dark secrets, are you, Anna?' The deep voice was teasing. 'That's not fair to poor downtrodden husbands.'

'Downtrodden!' Louise snorted. 'I'd like to see anyone big enough to try!'

'He wasn't always built like a giant,' Anna laughed up at him. 'When I first met him he was much more like Tom Thumb!'

'Enough! Enough! Isn't it time we were given a cup of tea?' Jacob protested.

'Tom Thumb?' Louise queried gently as Anna left to help supervise a round of hand-washing before the children went through to eat.

'She's exaggerating,' he dismissed huskily, as a dusky tide rose into his cheeks again.

'I'll make a bargain with you,' Louise offered as he

took her arm to lead her through to the other room.
'You can promise to tell me all about it later, yourself,
or I'll ask Anna to give me all the gory details.'

He laughed, his full baritone filling the hallway.

'I think it would be safer if I promised to tell you
myself.' He wrapped one arm around her shoulders
and pulled her into the warm strength of his body. 'At
least I might have a chance to find some way to distract
you.' And he lowered his head to steal a brief kiss.

# CHAPTER EIGHT

THE rest of their stay was hectic, with several clinics and another lengthy visit to the SCBU.

Louise had been thrilled to find herself accepted as a top-level professional, her opinions within her own field of expertise being accorded just as much weight as Jacob's were in his.

She was so preoccupied with everything she was seeing and learning and with trying to pass on her own skills that it didn't occur to her until they were already airborne on the return flight that she hadn't met a single member of Jacob's family.

The quiet glow which had surrounded her dimmed slightly as she wondered why he hadn't arranged a meeting.

As ever, she confided her thoughts to her diary, confident that Jacob was far too busy completing his notes to notice what she was doing. 'Is it because he's ashamed of me?' she wrote, then gazed out of the window at the billowing clouds wondering how she was going to ask.

'No,' a husky voice breathed into her ear, and she turned to find him leaning over her, his cheek all but touching hers, their lips just a heartbeat apart.

'What. . .?' She was mesmerised by the laser intensity of his sapphire-blue gaze.

'I said, no—in answer to the question you just wrote in your diary. It's not because I'm ashamed of you. Far from it. I couldn't be more proud of you.' And he leant forward that vital distance to stroke his lips lingeringly over hers.

Endless moments later she surfaced, her pulse fluttering at the base of her throat and her breathing decidedly unsteady.

'Then why?' It was an effort to remember what they had been talking about.

'Why what?' His concentration didn't seem to be any better than hers.

'Why didn't you introduce me to your family?' She tried hard but the hurt still showed in her voice.

Two hands came up to cup her face, his thumbs stroking the curve of her cheeks as if he loved the sensation. He fixed his gaze on her intently, his voice low and compelling.

'You met my *real* family. The ones I care about; the ones who care about me.' And his tone was so final that she knew he was not going to tell her anything further at the moment.

Maybe later.

Maybe when they knew each other well enough to learn to trust; perhaps he would tell her then why his eyes had looked so empty when he spoke about his family.

Before Louise had the chance to bring the subject up, Jacob mentioned her wish to return part-time to SCBU.

They had cleared the table after their evening meal and were starting the washing-up together in the kitchen. Jacob had rolled his sleeves up towards his elbows, revealing a large amount of well-muscled forearm.

Louise was watching him out of the corner of her eye as he picked up a glass and deftly began to dry it. She marvelled that just watching him perform an ordinary task like washing-up had started to arouse her and wondered if she was turning into some sort of sex fiend.

Jacob continued to work calmly, and she was glad he was unaware of her thoughts.

'The trip to Holland was very successful,' he commented in his usual calm way.

'Well, I certainly enjoyed myself. It was fantastic to have the chance to compare notes with others in the same field.' Louise knew her enthusiasm showed and was proud of it.

'The trip also proved that your idea about returning to St Augustine's should work quite well without short-changing Aletta,' he continued evenly.

'So, what are you suggesting,' Louise asked, her heart lifting with pleasure.

'Well, I thought it might be a good idea for you to say you will go back as a part-timer. You could take some of the load in the unit while you help train some of the new recruits. Later on, when we see how it all works out for Aletta, we can make any further decisions.'

'Oh, Jacob, thank you.' She threw her arms round his neck and aimed an impulsive kiss upwards towards his chin.

At the last moment he lowered his head and her lips met his, moist and open, in an aeons-long kiss which left them both breathless and shaking.

'I like the way you say thank you,' he rumbled hoarsely as he abandoned his cloth on the draining-board and swung her up into his arms.

Washing-up was totally forgotten as he carried her swiftly up the stairs, his head descending at intervals to nibble and tease.

Almost before they reached the bedroom her hands

were roaming the strong column of his neck, her fingers luxuriating in the silky profusion of his silver-blond hair.

The collar of his shirt was an unwelcome hindrance and she tried to unfasten the buttons even as he was lowering her to the broad expanse of the Emperor-sized bed.

'Louise,' he groaned as she ran her nails through the furring of his chest, tormenting the erect points of his dusky male nipples.

Desperation overtook them both as they disposed of each other's clothing and flung it helter-skelter around the room before sprawling together across the bed.

After the arid experience of her marriage to Colin, Louise was constantly amazed that Jacob needed to do little more than look at her for her to be desperate to make love with him.

The silence was broken only by the harsh sound of Jacob's unsteady gasps as Louise slid her hands down over the taut plane of his belly to capture his powerful heat in both hands.

'Jacob,' she moaned her pleasure as he flung one heavy thigh across her.

He paused, gazing down at her with burning eyes for long, tense seconds before he slid both arms around her and rolled over on to his back.

Their swift ascent into ecstasy left them both boneless with pleasure so that Louise found herself feeling rather guilty when she wished that Jacob had followed his first intention. She knew that he had wanted to straddle her in the age-old position of male dominance. Nothing would have pleased her more, but he still insisted on avoiding the possibility of overwhelming her.

How was she going to let him know that she trusted him implicitly without revealing that she had fallen in love with him. As usual she confided in the closely written pages of her diary.

If only, if only he could love me as much as I love him. Maybe, if he did, I might dare. . . Oh, God, how I would love to have his baby! To carry it in my body, to nurture it and then suckle it the way I do Aletta. But I can't. I daren't. I lost everything when I had Matthew, and I couldn't bear for it to happen again. It would be so much worse this time.

Louise hurried along the corridor, checking the time as she went.

Aletta had settled into the nursery as happily as if she had been there before. It was not the little girl's fault that Louise was rushing to arrive in SCBU on time.

At the last moment, when it was time to walk away from her, Louise had felt guilty—as if she really *was* deserting her, and had lingered just those few moments too long.

As her hand came up to push the door open, she caught sight of a familiar pair of shoulders through the glass panel.

Jacob turned towards her as he heard her enter the unit, his eyes searching her face carefully before he nodded briefly.

'J. . .' She paused, uncertain how she should address the consultant paediatrician who also happened to be her husband.

'Good morning, Staff Nurse,' he greeted her gravely, the smile in his eyes touching her like a caress before he turned towards the bustle of activity around a tiny unconscious body.

He was still there after she returned from hand-over, a worried frown pleating his forehead.

'Staff Nurse Su Yuen will fill you in on the details as you go along, but this little scrap has just come up to us from Theatre. Apparently the mother's latest boyfriend objected to being woken in the night and threw the baby against the wall. . .'

Louise gasped in horror. Although she had heard many such stories since she started nursing, especially since she decided to take her Registered Sick Children's Nurse certificate, each one sickened her anew.

'Quite.' His voice was clipped and he seemed outwardly detached, but Louise was learning to recognise the telltale signs of the deep emotions he kept so well hidden.

'It was a depressed skull fracture, so neurosurgery had to handle it. We're avoiding antibiotic prevention since it only encourages drug-resistant strains.'

'Oxygenation?' Louise queried briskly, squashing her emotional response.

'Forty per cent. Nurse Long has started setting up the inhalation positive pressure breathing machinery, but I'll check the settings myself. Poor little scrap is deeply comatose and he needs IPPB for the moment.'

'What are his chances? How soon are we going to be able to tell the degree of permanent damage?' Her heart had gone out to the tiny innocent victim.

'We won't know what his chances of recovery are until he starts showing signs of consciousness. Anything over a week is usually not very good news.' He sighed deeply and shook his head. 'I'll never understand how people can do such things to these helpless creatures.'

He turned towards her and reached for her hand, meshing his long tanned fingers with her daintier olive-toned ones.

'It's hard enough for them just to survive birth and the struggle of the first year of life. Then they're starved, beaten, abused, abandoned. . . Don't people realise that they have been entrusted with the preservation of our future?' His deep voice was pitched softly but that didn't alter the strength of his passionate belief in what he was saying.

Louise squeezed his hand, her throat almost too tight to allow her to speak.

'I shall have to make sure that Aletta knows exactly how lucky she is to have you for her daddy,' she whispered, her eyes bright with emotional tears. 'I wish all children could be so lucky. . .'

She felt the potent strength in his hand as he squeezed her fingers gently, then he stilled, raising her hand towards him.

'Where is your ring? Your wedding-ring?' His tone was sharp, almost accusatory.

With her free hand she reached into the neckline of her uniform to retrieve a slender gold chain, pulling it out to disclose the softly gleaming circle.

'I never feel right wearing jewellery when I'm on duty, but I couldn't bear to leave it at home. . .' She stopped speaking suddenly but it was already too late. She blushed as she realised how revealing her words were.

'I'm glad you feel that way. It makes me wonder if——'

A monitor bleeped sharply and they both turned towards the sound.

'Oh, no! Not Hannah again,' Louise muttered as she hurried forward to check the leads which snaked off in all directions from the nearly naked body.

'False alarm,' she sighed a minute later after she had checked everything over. 'I'm glad for the patients' sake that these things are fail-safe and make a noise whatever happens, but when you get one like "hasty Hannah" here, it can get very wearing.'

'Still, better safe than sorry,' Jacob agreed, checking the time on the wall clock. 'Today we're both due to finish at the same time, so whoever is free first can go up for Aletta and the other one can meet them there.'

He smiled down at her and turned to take a couple of paces towards the door before he stopped and retraced his steps.

'Have a good day,' he murmured rather self-consciously. Bending swiftly he dropped a kiss sweetly on her startled mouth before he hurried out of the unit.

Louise hoped for his sake that she was the only one who had seen the tide of red on the back of his neck and turned back to find a row of grinning faces confronting her.

'Wow!' teased Su Yuen. 'Was that the Mr den Haag we all know and love?'

'What have you done to him?' chimed in Carol Long from her position in the other corner of the room. 'He's as gorgeous as ever, but he always used to be such a cold fish.'

Louise felt the heat rising in her cheeks as she replayed in her mind the passionate kisses with which he had woken her just this morning. Jacob den Haag was no cold fish.

'I don't really remember what he was like before,' she answered candidly. 'Perhaps it's the effect of having a daughter that's changed him.'

Su Yuen blew a raspberry at that idea. 'The old Mr den Haag would never have dreamed of kissing anyone in public. I think it's your influence on him.'

'Nonsense,' Louise denied the accusation while she heard in her head Jacob's voice claiming that she was a bad influence on him, seducing him into wanting to stay in bed with her.

She felt the heat returning to her face and knew the only way to combat it was to keep her mind and hands occupied.

Jacob seemed distracted when they made their way home later that day, checking his watch and muttering under his breath about mountains of paperwork and hospital administration committees.

'Today of all days,' he added cryptically.

'Calm down, Jacob. It didn't matter that you got held up. It's all part of the job. Anyway,' she added, 'I had plenty of time to feed Aletta so she's not worried about being late home.'

'I wouldn't mind if I had been held up by a patient. I regard that as essential and unavoidable. It's the interminable piles of paper that get me down.'

'Jacob. . .' She got no further.

'Surely,' he continued forcefully, 'there are people intelligent enough to be trained to run a hospital without wasting doctors' time. They should be left to get on with their job.'

'It does make you wonder, sometimes,' Louise murmured quietly, knowing herself exactly how much time could be spent on work other than nursing.

'And then they want the doctors to waste precious hours on administration too!'

Jacob was scowling fiercely as he turned into their road but suddenly his face cleared as if by magic and he muttered almost inaudibly, 'At least one thing has gone right today,' and drew up behind a very new-looking small white saloon car parked almost outside their front gate.

'Wait here a minute,' he directed as he unclipped his belt. 'I just need to see if something's been delivered or whether there's a note about collection. . .'

Louise watched as he took the shallow front steps two at a time, his front door key ready in his hand.

She was puzzled when he opened the door and bent to pick something up off the mat inside the door without even entering the house and then closing the door to return to the car.

'Right.' He was smiling broadly as he opened her door. 'Hold these for me, will you?' He handed her a set of keys and turned to open the back door to release the cot restraint to lift Aletta out.

'You will find that those keys will open the doors on the car in front of us. Would you unlock it, please?'

Mystified, Louise obeyed then assisted Jacob in strapping Aletta into the carrycot restraint installed in the back seat.

'Now,' Jacob said, a hint of glee in his voice, 'if you would like to get in the driver's seat, you can take us for a quick trip in your new car.'

Louise stared at him over the gleaming roof of the car in amazement, her feet rooted to the pavement.

'*My* car? But. . .' She was speechless.

'You will need the car for travelling to and from the hospital. We can't always count on starting and finishing together.'

'But, I could have taken the bus. It's a direct route.'

'I know. But it's not such a good idea with Aletta to carry. And what if it rains?'

'Well. . .it seems such an extravagance, to have two cars when we'll be working at the same place.'

'Would it make any difference if we called it my wedding-gift to you?'

'No!' She heard her voice echo off the front of the row of houses and realised they were holding a lengthy conversation over the top of the car.

Bending down, she checked that Aletta was content then slid into the driver's seat. For several moments after Jacob shut the door on the passenger side they sat in silence, then Louise turned, a pained expression on her face.

'That sounded very ungracious and I didn't mean it that way.'

'Doesn't no mean no however you say it?' His voice was sombre and his face wore the closed expression she thought had gone for ever.

'No, it doesn't,' she objected forcefully. 'I love the car and I think it was wonderfully generous of you to buy it for me, but not as a wedding present.'

'Why not,' he demanded baldly.

'Because. . .because I can't give you a present.' The fire had gone out of her voice and she sounded mournful.

'Ah, Louise.' One warm hand cupped her cheek and turned her face up to meet his gaze. 'Don't you know you have given me something I have needed for more years than I like to remember. You have given me a family of my own.' His voice was husky and so unmistakably sincere that her own throat closed up emotionally.

'Oh, Jacob,' she whispered as she slid her fingers through the errant lock of silvery hair, stroking it back over his head until her hand curved around to urge him closer.

Their lips met softly in a fleeting kiss as light as the touch of thistledown.

They parted to gaze at each other and Louise felt as if her heart would overflow with love.

'Oh, I do l——' She stopped just in time before the words of love were uttered, and waited to see if he had guessed.

'What. . .?'

'I do l-like my little car.' She managed to drag her eyes away and concentrated on putting the key in the ignition. 'Where shall we go?'

'How about going over the route to the hospital just so that you can become accustomed to the gears? It's not as if you aren't capable of driving.'

Louise let out a silent sigh. It looked as if she had covered up her near slip, but. . .when Jacob had spoken to her like that it had been almost impossible not to tell him how she felt.

Please, God, let him fall in love with me. Soon! She sent her thoughts winging upwards. Otherwise I might explode while I'm waiting!

'It's funny,' Louise mused aloud as she sat up in bed writing her diary.

'What is?' Jacob's deep voice made her jump.

'Oh! You surprised me,' she exclaimed. 'I thought you were still down in your study lost under an avalanche of paperwork!'

He strolled over to sit down on the edge of the bed and leant forward to brush a kiss over her forehead.

'I'd had enough of it.' He linked his fingers together behind his head and stretched widely, his shirt-tails pulling out of his trousers to reveal a band of taut flesh bisected by a silky line of hair which disappeared beneath the waistband.

Her fingers clenched with the need to follow the line

to its destination and she heard him draw in a sharp
breath.

'Louise. . .' Her eyes met his and she was scorched
by the heat. 'When you look at me like that, I can't
help myself. I just want to. . .' He abandoned speech
in favour of action, lifting her effortlessly into his arms
and turning so that they lay side by side, his hands
roaming intimately over every inch of her body.

'You are so soft, so sweet, so sexy.' His lips followed
the trails his hands had blazed, making sure that she
was fully aroused before taking his pleasure, proving
once again that he was the most gentle and considerate
of lovers.

Louise lay awake for some time after Jacob had
relaxed into sleep. In her mind she was conducting a
futile argument between the side of herself which
had never known such ecstasy and the side which
wished Jacob, too, would relax his fierce control over
himself.

Unfortunately, she knew she didn't yet have the
courage to ask him to lower his guard, nor did she
know how to provoke it herself.

Sometimes a man could be too careful, too considerate when a woman just wanted to be made love to as
if there were nothing more important in the world.

Louise had woken early that morning and had taken
the chance to write a few extra lines, her late-night
thoughts lingering on in her mind.

It is one of the most elemental and basic acts
between two people—the means of survival of the
whole human race, and it should feel like that—as
if each act is the miracle which starts the existence
of another human being. . . Oh, God, if only I
dared. . .

Aletta stirred and Louise put the pen down quickly to pick her up before she disturbed Jacob.

Later, in the last-minute rush to check that she had left everything tidy, she knocked the diary and pen flying to land at Jacob's feet.

He crouched smoothly to retrieve them, glancing idly at the cover.

'How long have you been keeping a diary?' he asked, placing it in her outstretched hand.

'A long time——' she smiled reminiscently '—probably ever since I learnt to write.'

'What do you write? A list of appointments, the events of the day, or is it your confidante? Do you tell it all your hopes and dreams?'

Louise laughed. 'There's a bit of all three at times, but it started off as a sort of letter to an imaginary friend.'

She went to slip it into the drawer of the bedside cabinet but it jammed against something already in the drawer. She fished inside and pulled out a framed photograph which she fumbled to hide.

'Secrets?' Jacob teased, his eyes suddenly laser-sharp on the touch of colour which crept over the olive of her cheeks.

'N. . . No, not really. It's just. . .' Silently she held out the photograph which had been taken of Matthew when he was only hours old.

'Ah, Louise.' Jacob stepped forward to draw her into his arms. 'Why do you keep this *inside* the drawer?' He turned the frame so that they were both looking at the photo. 'If you want to put it where you can see it, I will not mind. I knew him too, remember?'

Louise looked up at him, tears of gratitude sparkling in the corners of her eyes then, from the comfort of Jacob's embrace, she looked down at the photo again.

With one shaky finger she traced the mop of straight dark hair and around the curve of one baby cheek. The photographer had caught Matthew with his eyes wide open, their dark colour, nearly jet-black in the photo, giving him such a serious expression.

'His colouring was quite a bit darker than yours, especially his hair,' Jacob mused. 'I can remember thinking that the contrast made the similarities in your features all the more remarkable.'

Louise had tensed, unable to help her reaction. Jacob obviously noticed, but before he could remark on it the phone rang.

After an initial greeting, Jacob switched to Dutch.

Louise busied herself collecting Aletta's bag of essentials and returned with her to stand beside Jacob, not wanting to leave without saying goodbye.

'*Een ogenblik, meneer.*' He turned to Louise, leaning forward to stroke his daughter's cheek briefly. 'You'd better go on. I don't know how long this call will take.' He kissed her, his free hand cradling her head as his lips opened over hers and stole her breath away.

'Drive carefully,' he whispered, giving her a last peck on the tip of her nose.

That had been the last pleasant interlude of the day.

Louise had arrived in the unit just as a five-day-old baby boy was brought into the unit with meningitis.

She swung into action as she read his notes.

'Fresh frozen plasma is on its way up, Kate,' she directed the newest recruit to the unit. 'As soon as it arrives, set the drip-rate for thirty millilitres over three hours, and call me to check it.'

Within minutes she was back at her side to approve her conscientious work.

'Any questions?' she offered, taking an immediate

liking to Kate Barker's calm air and willingness to learn.

'Do we know how the meningitis was diagnosed?' she ventured.

'According to the notes, Mother's membranes ruptured twelve hours before active labour started and the baby had to be resuscitated on arrival. All seemed well and as she has two others at home the mother insisted on going home after three days. About six hours ago, he started having seizures so Mother brought him in.'

Kate nodded, concentrating intently.

'In A and E she said that he'd been vomiting and had diarrhoea, and you can see for yourself that he's quite jaundiced. Mother apparently put it down to a change in brand of milk formula.'

'But. . .' the younger woman hesitated.

'What?' Louise prompted. 'If you've got a question, ask. It's the only way to learn,' she smiled encouragingly.

'Well, none of those things seems terribly serious, and they could be caused by lots of different things.'

'Good girl! Quite right!' Louise praised and saw Kate pinken with pleasure. 'Examining the cerebrospinal fluid was the final confirmation.'

'What did they find in the CSF and what can they do about it?'

'Gram-negative E. coli showed up, so he's on a corticosteroid to reduce the inflammation and an antibiotic——' she checked the notes '——to combat the E. coli.'

'But that's the same stuff my flatmate was given for a candida infection!'

'That's the wonder of science!' Louise joked.

For several hours it looked as if the child was rallying and Louise was kept busy supervising Kate as she checked the little mite's vital signs as well as chasing up some missing supplies.

'Thank goodness we've built up a reserve stock,' she muttered to Su Yuen as she rang through to the children's ward in the vain hope that their supplies had turned up there. 'If not, we could be desperate by now.'

Her own charge, Hannah, had developed some worrying shadows on her X-rays and, with the little patient in Holland so clear in her memory, Louise found her thoughts drawn towards the theatre where Hannah had been taken for exploratory surgery.

After the trauma of seeing their unconscious daughter off, Louise had taken Hannah's parents through to Sister's office for a cup of tea and then had directed them to the nearby chapel.

'It's not just a religious place,' she quickly explained when Hannah's father looked as if he would object. 'It's somewhere peaceful where you can get away from the noise of other people and just be together.'

She remembered the hours she had spent in there herself while she tried to come to terms with the destruction of her storybook happy ending.

'Some people prefer to go to the park,' Louise continued. 'It's just round the corner from the hospital main entrance, but it's so cold and wet today. . .'

Hannah's mother looked up at her husband and smiled wanly as he nodded.

Louise squeezed her arm gently as they turned to go.

'I'll send someone to get you as soon as she comes back to the unit,' she promised as they left.

\*     \*     \*

Jacob had just arrived in the unit to check up on their little patient with meningitis when Hannah returned.

Kate had called Louise over when she made her last check on his vital signs. There had been a sudden marked deterioration and Louise had immediately called for the paediatrician on duty.

She had shown Jacob the recent figures and he leant over the silent figure to start his own assessment.

Before anyone could draw breath the monitor started emitting the ominous tone which indicated cardiac arrest.

All eyes were drawn instantly to the sinister lack of movement in the tiny chest. Simultaneously they moved, each to their respective tasks in a well-rehearsed drill.

'Atropine sulphate. . .' Jacob rapped out as Louise simultaneously placed the prepared syringe in his outstretched hand.

When he began resuscitation Louise was reminded in graphic detail just how large a man he was, his hands dwarfing the tiny chest he was working on.

Without a word being spoken between them, Louise found that she and Jacob had synchronised their work perfectly. Even so, when several further attempts to stimulate the heart chemically failed, and after more than fifteen minutes of concentrated effort, Jacob reached his hand out to cover hers.

'It's no good,' he muttered hoarsely as he shook his head, his eyes dark and empty with failure, and he leant across to disconnect the leads.

'Oh, God. . .!' Jacob and Louise turned simultaneously to the source of the wail.

Hannah's parents were standing in the doorway to the unit, their faces ashen.

'My baby!' Mrs Lloyd keened. 'My baby!' and she

stumbled towards them. 'I didn't even say goodbye. . .'
And her hands reached out in despair.

'No, Mrs Lloyd.' Louise stepped swiftly forward to
intercept her and turned her towards the cot which
had been pushed aside in the recent flurry of activity.
'*This* is Hannah.'

'Oh, God,' she breathed, stopping beside her
daughter and hanging on to the side of her cot as if
she had no strength to stand unaided. 'Thank you,
God. I couldn't bear it if she had gone without. . .'
She gulped and swiped ineffectually at her tearstained
cheeks.

Jacob leant towards Louise and murmured gently,
'Give them a few minutes to calm down, then bring
them through to Sister's room.'

Her eyes lifted to his, her own filled with the
unspoken question.

He shook his head silently, sadly, and her heart fell.

She watched as he drew in a deep breath, inflating
his broad chest fully before releasing it. He looked so
tired, so discouraged, so much in need of comfort.

# CHAPTER NINE

LOUISE held a cloth soaked in cold water against her swollen eyelids.

She had managed to hold out until she had finished her shift, but once she had shut the front door behind her the dam had burst.

Kate had been the first to crack. Louise had heard her sobbing in the sluice.

'Was it my fault?' she cried against Louise's shoulder when she went in to comfort her. 'Should I have spotted something sooner?'

'No, Kate.' Louise shook her gently. 'You did everything you should. It caught us all by surprise.' She grabbed a handful of paper towel and passed it to Kate to mop up. 'The statistics aren't good in neonatal meningitis. The mortality rate is still about sixty percent. Even when they survive, three quarters of them have severe central nervous system dysfunctions such as hydrocephalus.'

'So his chances weren't very good?'

'If he'd been brought in sooner, he might have had a better chance of surviving. But that's an emotional response. We don't like losing a patient.' She smiled sadly, remembering her own desperation—wanting Matthew to live so badly. . .'Sometimes, though,' she went on, 'it's kinder to the baby to let him go with love. . .'

'I'm sorry I let it all get on top of me. How do you manage not to let it get to you? Does it come with experience?'

'I wish it did,' Louise's expression was wry. 'In the end we all find our own ways of coping—we have to, otherwise we'd go round the bend.'

Having assured herself that Kate had recovered, Louise went into the unit to take Mr and Mrs Lloyd through to Sister's office.

Jacob had anticipated her and a tray of freshly brewed tea was waiting on the desk. He ushered the couple into chairs and then sat down himself, knowing that his great height would be intimidating enough without the news he had to impart.

He had signalled for Louise to stay and, after handing round cups of tea, she sat herself on the small upright chair in the corner.

'It's not good, is it?' Mr Lloyd took the bull by the horns. 'She hasn't put on any more weight and her charts all show she's weaker than she was before.'

'You're right, Mr Lloyd.' Jacob's baritone was filled with compassion. 'The exploratory operation shocked us.'

'Why?' Mrs Lloyd's voice was a reedy quiver, the cup she held rattling so badly in the saucer that she had to put it down. 'You thought she might have this NEC. . .?'

'Necrotising enterocolitis,' Jacob confirmed. 'Yes. There were shadows on the last set of X-rays and we were hoping that the affected sections of her intestines could be removed and still leave her with enough for recovery.'

'So what went wrong?' Mr Lloyd was starting to sound belligerent.

'When they opened her up, it was everywhere,' Jacob said simply. 'We don't understand how she is still alive.' He shook his head in puzzlement.

'What do you mean?' Mrs Lloyd whispered.

'The amount of damage she has inside her system, she should have gone into septic shock long ago. She should never have survived the anaesthetic, never mind the operation.'

'Then what's going on?' Mr Lloyd's anger had gone. Now he just sounded bewildered.

'If I may, Mr den Haag?' Louise broke in softly from her unobtrusive seat in the corner.

He fixed his gaze on her intently for a moment, then nodded and gestured for her to join them.

Louise came over and knelt down in front of Mrs Lloyd, taking the hand not being held by her husband between both of her own.

'Your Hannah has been a little fighter right from the moment she was born, hasn't she?' Mrs Lloyd smiled tearfully and glanced at her husband.

'You and your husband have spent endless hours in the unit, willing her to succeed, praising her for every little gain, each step forward.

'I think——' Louise took a steadying breath, feeling the tears come perilously close 'I—think she's waiting for you to give her permission to let go; to stop fighting.' She swallowed hard and focused on Mr Lloyd. 'I think she needs you to tell her she's fought long enough. You'll never forget her—we'll never forget her either——' she included Jacob in her gaze '—but now she needs to find peace.'

There was a long silence in the room broken only by the sound of Mrs Lloyd's stifled sobs.

'Would you like us to leave you alone for a while to talk?' Jacob offered, preparing to rise from his chair.

'No,' Mr Lloyd's voice wavered a little, but it was decisive. He turned to his wife. 'She's right, isn't she, love?' he spoke softly. 'Hannah's been a little battler but it's time to tell her enough is enough.'

He stood and helped her out of her seat.

'Please.' Mrs Lloyd's eyes were fixed beseechingly on Jacob. 'Just this last time. . .can we hold her? Without all those tubes and wires. . .?' She drew in a shuddering breath. 'I just want to feel that she's ours. . .just for a few minutes. . .'

'Of course you can,' he agreed gently. 'Staff Nurse will go through with you as soon as you're ready. . .'

Louise heard Jacob coming in the front door just as she was putting Aletta to bed.

'Sleep tight, precious,' she whispered, kissing the downy head and smoothing the covers over her.

'Asleep already?' the baritone rumble came softly over her shoulder.

'Yes. I'm sorry you missed your cuddle with her but she couldn't keep her eyes open any longer.' Louise was resting her hands on the side of the cot looking down at the sleeping child. She knew that as soon as she turned, Jacob would be able to tell that she had been crying.

She felt his breath on her cheek as he leant forward to stroke Aletta's cheek and took her chance, turning away from the circle of his arm and stepping quickly across to the door.

'Louise. . .?' he called gently, and she paused with her hand on the door. 'I envy you. . .' The soft words were so unexpected that she forgot her reason for trying to escape and turned to face him.

'Envy me?' She was puzzled. 'What on earth for?'

His eyes were deep sapphire pools and as he walked towards her she felt as if she was drowning in their depths.

He cradled her face between his large warm palms and gazed at her intently.

'I envy the fact that you are able to release your tension and pain in tears. I have never been able to do this.'

'You find it very difficult to relinquish control,' she agreed, the careful watch she kept on her tongue less stringent in the aftermath of her tears. 'You like to be in command of yourself all the time, even when we. . .'

She dragged her eyes away from his in horror as she realised what she had nearly said.

'Come.' He took her arm and led her out of Aletta's room and into their own, pushing the door shut and switching on the intercom which would allow them to hear her if she woke.

Louise felt herself start to tremble in trepidation at what she had implied, then gave herself a mental shake. It was no more than the truth, so why shouldn't she say it?

'It's true, you know.' She turned to face him, her chin tilted upwards in defiance. 'Even in here you always have to direct everything.' One arm swept out wildly to indicate the emperor-sized bed in the elegant bedroom as weeks of disappointment finally came to a head. 'Are you afraid to trust me? Do you think I might try to hurt you while you're out of control for a few minutes?'

'No!' His tone was agonised. 'Louise, no! It is not like that. *Jij begrijpt het niet!*' He finally lost his command of English completely, raking both hands through his hair in his frustration before swinging her up in his arms in a fierce embrace.

The silk robe she had donned after her shower fluttered wildly with the swift movement and Louise held on to his shoulders till her head stopped spinning, then took the opportunity to look him straight in the eye.

'Then why,' she demanded equally fiercely. 'Tell

me.' And she thumped his chest with both fists.

'Hey!' The surprise of her attack seemed to break the tension in both of them. 'Pick on someone your own size!'

'I was always told that the bigger they are, the harder they fall.' She tapped him again, then slid her open palms over his shoulders to link them in the silky hair at the back of his neck. 'Talk to me, Jacob,' she pleaded. 'I need to know what you're feeling.'

He drew in a deep breath and she felt the muscles of his chest expand impressively. He carried her across and sat on the side of the bed, turning her until she was sitting on his lap, firmly held in the circle of his powerful arms, her head resting against his chest so that she could hear the steady beat of his heart.

'From when I am. . .' he corrected himself '. . .when I was little. . .'

'Jacob,' she interrupted gently, placing one finger on his lips to silence him. 'Just speak to me. I'll let you know if I don't understand.'

'OK,' he nodded and she felt him relax his shoulders. 'When I started to grow so big, I was told that I must always be careful or I will hurt someone. Then, when I was married to Aletta's mother. . . No,' he interrupted himself, '*you* are Aletta's mother; she was only the woman who carried her. Anyway she, too, said this to me. That I am too big, too clumsy. That I am like big animal and I will hurt her if we make love.'

'But Jacob, I told you that *I* don't feel that way about you, and you took no notice.' She snatched a breath and decided that bluntness might be best. 'You are a wonderful lover and you have never hurt me. Not once. But. . .I want it all. I want you to make love with me any way that feels right for us.'

He held her by her shoulders and leant her back

slightly, running his eyes over her. 'But you are so small. It is not possible for us. . .for me to. . .to. . .' A tide of colour spread upwards.

'How do we know what we are capable of if we never try? Life is full of surprises, good and bad, and there is usually some sort of balance. Sometimes we have to take chances or we would miss out on the most rewarding things of all.'

Jacob was silent for a long time, absent-mindedly stroking her hair as he rocked slowly back and forth.

'Today wasn't a good day in the unit.' She heard the rumble of his voice through the wall of his chest as she snuggled against him.

'I wouldn't like to go through another one like that for a long time,' she agreed quietly.

'That was a wonderful thing you did for Hannah's parents.' The pride in his voice was unmistakable.

'Wonderful?' she questioned. 'There's nothing wonderful about a child dying.'

'Ah, but the *way* of her dying. You made it something so special between them. You saw it yourself.'

Louise felt the tears building up behind her eyes. 'It brought it all back. . . Matthew dying. First the little boy with meningitis, then Hannah. Sometimes it feels as if the whole world is dying and I'm powerless to do anything but try to make the dying a little easier.'

'Then I must do my best to make sure you realise that we are alive and life is for living.' His voice became progressively husky as she turned her face up towards his.

'*Liefste*,' he murmured huskily. '*Mijn liefste. . .*'

Then he dipped his head and kissed her.

The movements of his mouth were slow and seductive. He courted and coaxed, never asking for more than Louise was eager to surrender.

'J-Jacob,' she whispered shakily when the kiss finally came to an end. 'Oh, Jacob. . .'

She lifted her hand to stroke the lean plane of his cheek, her thumb tracing the ridge of his cheekbone and down over the rasp of new beard growth until it came to the corner of his mouth.

She paused for a second or two, examining the slightly swollen outline of his lips before she tested them with a slow stroke of the pad of her thumb.

They parted and she felt the moist warmth of his breath against her, followed by the teasing lick of his tongue.

He gathered her close and she was made unmistakably aware of the potent thrust of his arousal.

His hands explored the sleek silk-covered lines of her thighs and the womanly swell of her hips then stroked upwards, slipping between the overlapped layers of her robe and dislodging the precarious knot which held them together.

Louise was trembling with anticipation by the time he finally caressed his way to her breasts. He cupped them gently, feathering her nipples with the sensitive pads of his thumbs until they were darkly swollen.

'Jacob!' she cried out when he finally touched the aching passion-engorged peaks with the searing heat of his mouth. The sensation that arrowed through her into her depths in that first instant of contact was so intense it was almost agony.

They kissed again, deeply, demandingly.

Louise slid her hands down from their preoccupation with the live silk of his hair and brought them over his shoulders to attack the buttons of his shirt.

She spread the edges open with an impatient gesture and furrowed her fingers through the warm pelt which covered his chest in an inverted triangle, searching out the flat coppery discs and tormenting them in return.

'Louise!' he groaned, evading her attentions just long enough to discard his shirt then hauling her into his arms again, lifting her effortlessly to lay her down on the bed.

Her robe slithered aside leaving her totally naked to his avid gaze.

'*Mooi. Heel mooi*,' he whispered huskily.

As his sapphire gaze travelled from the pouting glory of her engorged breasts to the shadowy secrets of the delta of dark gold curls that clustered between her thighs it was as if he drew his fingers over her.

Muscles deep within her body contracted in response.

'Now it's your turn,' she murmured, her words drawing his eyes up to mesh with her own. 'Take your clothes off, Jacob, I want to look at you, too.'

He was still for a moment, as if he could not believe what he had heard her say.

'*In's hemelsnaam*!' he exclaimed, his hands clenched tightly into fists, then they were moving, fumbling in his haste to unfasten his trousers.

Finally, he stood exposed and vulnerable to her, the dark colour in his cheeks evidence of his self-consciousness.

'Come here,' she invited with a beckoning hand. 'It isn't enough just to look. . .'

And he was there beside her, his mouth taking hers in a kiss of overwhelming passion, his hands roaming her body, enticing, exciting, coaxing her nearer, caressing her more and more intimately.

Louise was helpless in her arousal, her hips shifting sinuously, arching provocatively.

'Please,' she breathed, reaching for his shoulders and raking them with her nails. 'Please, Jacob, now,' and she parted her thighs for him in mute demand.

She saw his pupils dilate until the sapphire-blue almost disappeared.

'Ah, Louise, my Louise,' he uttered passionately as, for the first time he shifted his body on to hers.

He held himself rigid, the weight of his upper body supported by his elbows.

'You will tell me if I am too heavy for you.'

'I would,' she agreed, 'if you *were* too heavy. As it is——' her voice grew sultry and her movements languid as she drew her knees up to clasp them around his hips '——you feel absolutely perfect.'

The explosive breath he had been holding teased the halo of curls circling her face, as he leant forward to bury his face in their softness.

'Please, Jacob, I need you,' she whispered. 'Show me how good life can be. . . Ahh!'

She had no need to ask him again. Her words had been the trigger which drove him to possess her, and in turn to surrender to her possession.

Which one of them set the rhythm for what followed was not important. Unconsciously they were totally in harmony with each other, striving together until they reached the pinnacle of consummation.

'Louise!' It was a triumphant shout, completely over-shadowing her breathless cry of ecstasy as the world went up in flames.

Long moments later Jacob lifted himself off her but not to move far.

'*Ik houd van jou, vrouw van me,*' he murmured softly as he curled his large body around hers protectively, one hand coming to rest on the soft hollow of her stomach.

'Tell me again. What does that mean,' she snuggled herself against his body, revelling in the closeness.

'Oh, it—er, it means. . .you're beautiful,' he said rather hesitantly.

'Thank you.' She smiled up at him, not caring that he might realise how much she loved him. At this precise moment she was too content to care. 'Can you say it to a man?'

'What do you mean?'

'I think you're beautiful, too, and I want to learn how to say that in Dutch,' she gazed up at him openly. 'Will you teach me the words you said?'

Jacob paused before he spoke, a strange expression crossing his face.

'I will teach you to say to me what I have been saying to you.'

Louise smiled when she heard his awkward phrasing, loving the exotic touch of his accent.

'You will say to me "*Ik hou van jou, man van me.*"' He spoke the words slowly and clearly so that she was able to copy his pronunciation at the first attempt.

'Was that right?'

'Perfect,' he complimented. 'Now all you have to do is practise saying it as if you mean it.'

'That will be easy,' she said, her eyes shining up at him. 'Because I do mean it. You are a beautiful man, on the inside as well as your body.' And she repeated the Dutch words he had taught her as if they were a sacred vow.

Next day she found herself confiding in her diary.

It was everything I always dreamt it could be. We were so much in harmony with each other that we didn't have to think how to please each other. This is happening so much between the two of us these days, as if we are growing closer together mentally as well as physically.

Perhaps, one day I will get up the courage to tell him why I'm so afraid to have his baby, but, oh, it couldn't possibly get any better than it was last night, even if we had been making love to make a baby.

She tucked the pen back in its slot down the spine of the diary and smoothed the tassel attached to its top between the pages to keep them flat.

When Jacob returned home that night he seemed unusually preoccupied.

Several times Louise started to ask him if anything was the matter but because she had a lingering fear that he was regretting letting down his guard with her, she held her tongue.

Suddenly, in the middle of a programme they usually watched together, he got up and left the room.

Louise listened intently and heard his footsteps go up the stairs and along the corridor to Aletta's door. There was a long silence and she had just decided to follow him to see what was wrong when she heard him move on into their room.

For some time it sounded as if he was pacing backwards and forwards then his footsteps halted in the region of her side of the bed.

Louise had lost all interest in the programme, her whole attention centering on Jacob and his strange mood.

When she finally went upstairs, she heard Jacob moving and the sound of a drawer closing but by the time she entered the room, he was in the bathroom turning on the shower.

Whatever had been bothering him had obviously been resolved because seconds later he appeared clothed only in a brief towel, wisps of steamy air following him as he walked towards her.

'I have decided that it would be a good idea for us to start being more economical,' he announced as he came to a halt in front of her.

'What. . .?'

'Shh.' He put one finger over her lips and continued, 'I think it is very wasteful for us to have two separate showers each evening when one lot of water will do.'

'Really?' Louise managed to choke out. 'And how thrifty are you being when you turn the shower on and leave it running?'

'Ah, but that's all your fault for lingering out here when the shower is all ready for you.' And he took her arm and led her mock-solicitously across the room.

Louise succumbed to a fit of the giggles as his towel slipped and threatened to drop completely, and then decided to give it a helping hand.

They had reached the bathroom by then and Jacob turned her towards himself at the same time as he pushed the door closed, leaning back against the door to pull her into his arms.

'Ah, Louise. Today has been far too long.' His voice was a heartfelt groan as he angled his head to fuse his mouth to hers.

The next couple of days seemed to be the start of a whole new phase in their life together. Before, Jacob had been gratifyingly keen to make love to her; now he was positively insatiable—and Louise found herself loving every minute of it.

She was learning for the first time the power she held in her hands. The power to tease and tempt, to excite and arouse and most of all, totally to satisfy the man she loved.

Each time they came together was better, more

fulfilling than the last, with Jacob insisting that they curl up together to prolong the afterglow.

In those lazy, languid times he would try to persuade her to talk about the hopes and wishes she'd had as a child. Eventually the time came when she admitted how much she had longed to have a baby.

'In some ways, the time when I was pregnant was the happiest time of my life.' Her voice was soft in the subdued light but she knew he could hear every word. 'It was a time filled with hope for the future. I made such plans. . .such foolish plans. . .'

'Were they so foolish?' he prompted. 'Surely you can see now that they are still possible?'

'Some of them, yes. I can look after Aletta and watch her grow as if she had always been mine. . .'

'But you know inside that she was not your child,' he finished too perceptively for her peace of mind. 'So? Why don't you do something about it? You must know that there is no reason why you shouldn't.'

'I don't know what you. . . Do you mean that. . . that you would let me adopt Aletta?'

'Do you want to?' His voice sounded almost startled, as if the thought hadn't occurred to him before she said it.

'Oh, Jacob, I'd love to,' she said fervently, then paused. 'But isn't that what you were suggesting?'

'No, Louise, although I'm delighted at the idea. No, what I meant was for you to have our baby.'

'No!' The shock of his suggestion turned her to stone. 'No. I can't,' she cried out, while a little voice inside her head screamed for her to say yes. 'I daren't,' she whispered finally, 'I daren't risk losing everything again.'

Jacob seemed stunned by her adamant reaction and

it took him several minutes to marshall his words.

'But, Louise,' he coaxed gently, 'you know about the recent research into spina bifida as well as I do. You take a folic acid supplement to raise the levels in the body before you try to start a pregnancy and continue taking it for the first few weeks. The results were almost miraculous in the research.'

'Nooo. . .' she moaned, the temptation almost more than she could withstand. How she would love to know that she was carrying Jacob's baby inside her. 'You don't understand. I'm so afraid. . .' And she turned away from him, curling into a small ball around the pain of longing for the very thing she couldn't have.

Jacob dropped the conversation, concentrating instead on soothing her until she relaxed, and then making love to her until she forgot everything except how much she loved her gentle giant.

Her work at the SCBU was so satisfying. Not only was she continuing to nurse in the specialist field she enjoyed so much, but now she was having the chance to pass her expertise on to other nurses.

Kate Barker and Julia Somerset were the first recruits. Each had already taken their Registered Sick Children's Nurse qualification and were working towards a greater degree of responsibility and deeper specialist knowledge.

'Julia Somerset is good,' she reported to Jacob one night after a particularly hectic day with two tiny babies coming in on blue lights from different directions within minutes of each other. 'She'll make a very competent SCBU nurse. But Kate Barker has got that special something. She's quick and hardworking, like Julia, but she's also intuitive. . .'

'In fact, she's not unlike you,' Jacob teased gently,

pulling her round to rest against him on the settee.

She reached up to plant a kiss at the angle of his jaw, feeling the rasp of his emerging beard against her lips.

'The only thing I worry about,' he continued as he wrapped both arms around her, 'is that you might be taking on too much. No——' he held up one hand to silence her when she would have objected '——I'm not criticising you. Not your work in the unit, which is as excellent as ever, nor your care of Aletta.'

'Well, then. What do you mean?'

'You know as well as I do that Aletta is growing up fast, and I know you make certain to spend a lot of time with her when you're at home. I just worry a little that you're burning the candle at both ends. If you get run down then you won't be able to do anything well.'

Louise was silent for a while as she thought over what he had said.

'You could be right,' she finally admitted. 'In fact, I have been wondering. . .'

'What?' he queried. 'Anything I can help with?'

'Well, I'm not certain whether I need to change my brand of Pill. . .' She felt him grow tense.

'Any particular reason?'

'I'm gradually weaning Aletta, so it's not such a problem if it interferes with my milk supply, but the present one seems to. . .I don't know.' She shook her head. 'It seemed all right at first, but just lately I've missed one period and my breasts have been rather tender.'

His hands came up to cradle them and then he slid her sweatshirt up to examine them further.

'They do seem slightly fuller than usual,' he commented as his fingers gently stroked their upper curves.

Soon her nipples began to harden and she looked up at him in time to see the absorbed look on his face change to a smile of purely masculine satisfaction.

'Ah, Louise, they're beautiful.' He cupped them again as though weighing them in the broad cradle of his palms. 'Are they too sensitive for me to touch them?' He lowered his head towards hers to tease her lips with a series of unsatisfying nibbles before she moaned her desire for more, all thoughts of pain submerged under a floodtide of pleasure.

The next morning, almost as soon as her eyes were open, Jacob had a suggestion to make.

'I was thinking about what you said last night—about your Pill.'

'Do you think it's possibile I need to change brands?'

'What I thought was that we could short-circuit the system to find out if it's necessary.'

'You mean, by checking the concentration in my system?'

'Right.'

'Do I need to make an appointment with the Family Planning Clinic, or what?'

'Actually, what I thought was that you could do a urine specimen when you get up this morning, and I'll take some blood before we leave for the hospital. I've got syringes and so on in my study. What do you think?' He seemed almost eager.

'You're in a ghoulish mood today, are you? Can't wait to get your first pint of blood,' she teased, and then squealed when he pretended to make a vampire attack on her neck.

Once he had taken the specimens, she put the whole matter out of her head, knowing that he would tell her the results as soon as they came through.

Halfway through her shift the next day they had a

call telling them of the whereabouts of the elusive supplies.

Louise volunteered to collect them, telling Sister Wilson that she wanted to look in on Aletta as she passed. She had seemed a little fretful that morning, and while Louise had a feeling it was just a touch of the miseries associated with teething, she wanted to check to set her mind at rest.

She was walking swiftly towards the bank of lifts when she recognised Jatinder Smith coming from the other direction, her hands full of the paraphernalia for taking blood samples. Louise knew her quite well as she was a frequent visitor to SCBU.

'I'm on my way down. What about you?' Louise's finger hovered over the buttons.

'Down for me, too, please.' She smiled, her dark eyes gleaming. 'These are all on their way to the lab for testing.'

The doors slid quietly shut then opened almost immediately as they reached Louise's destination.

'By the way, I hear congratulations are in order.' Jatinder spoke just as Louise was about to leave the lift. 'I'm so pleased for you.'

The doors started to close on her as she stood on the threshold and she reached in quickly to press the 'hold' button.

'Congratulations? What for?' Louise was mystified. She had seen Jatinder frequently since her marriage to Jacob, so what could she be talking about?

'Your pregnancy!' She sounded delighted.

'What. . .?' Louise was speechless. 'Who. . .?'

'Your husband brought the samples in to the lab. Of course, the results would normally go straight to him, as his name was on the request form, but as soon as I saw you I couldn't resist saying something. . .

Oh, no!' It had finally dawned on her that Louise's expression was totally blank. 'I've spoilt the surprise, haven't I?' she wailed. 'I never dreamt it was a secret. I'm so sorry. . .'

Louise shook her head and dredged a half smile up from somewhere. 'Don't worry, I promise I won't tell him it was you.'

The squeak of rubber soled shoes on composite flooring announced the arrival of another passenger, and Louise thankfully raised her hand in a brief farewell before turning away from the doors.

No! No! No! her mind was screaming numbly. It can't be true. There must be some mistake.

# CHAPTER TEN

HER feet carried her along the corridor to collect the missing supplies and she paused briefly to check from the doorway that Aletta was sleeping peacefully. She didn't dare go over to her or the temptation to grab her out of the cot and run might have overwhelmed her.

As it was, she returned to SCBU, outwardly as calm as she had left it just a quarter of an hour ago. Inside, she knew that calm, happy person had disappeared completely, trapped in the middle of a nightmare with no way out.

Within an hour the stress of concentrating on caring for her tiny charges while trying not to think of the decisions she was going to have to make when she returned home had given her a pounding headache.

'Louise.' Jenny Wilson stopped her as she passed the door to Sister's office. 'You're looking terribly pale. Are you sure you're feeling all right?'

Louise squeezed her eyes tight shut and took a deep breath.

'No, Sister. Actually, I'm not feeling very well.' Her eyelids felt weighted down with the pain in her head and she felt cold all over, even in the extra warmth of the unit.

'I think you'd be better off at home. If you're coming down with something we can't afford to spread it round the unit.'

Louise agreed gratefully, apologising for leaving them short-handed before she sped as fast as her head would allow to collect Aletta.

Driving was beyond her. Even the thought of concentrating on the other traffic on the road made her feel sick, so she was grateful to sink into the seat of the first taxi parked in the rank outside the hospital.

She cradled Aletta against her shoulder, smoothing her cheek over the baby's silky head, grateful for the feel of her warmth, breathing in the familiar sweet baby smell.

And all the time her mind was racing, racing. Thoughts and ideas, hopes and dreams all colliding with the sheer terror of her worst nightmare.

Aletta settled down happily after her feed, seemingly unaware of Louise's turmoil.

She'd had to force herself to put the baby to bed when all her instincts were screaming at her to hold on to her as long as possible. She knew, though, that she had some serious thinking to do, some decisions to make before Jacob came home.

The phone rang. Louise nearly reached out to answer it then remembered that the answering machine was still switched on.

She was glad she had let the machine take the call when she heard Jacob's familiar deep voice after the bleep.

'Louise. It's Jacob. Jenny Wilson told me you had to go home. Give me a ring to let me know how you are. . .' There was a long pause after he finished speaking before he quietly put the phone down.

'What am I going to do?' She wailed the words aloud and heard them reverberate around the room.

In her desire to preserve her milk supply for Aletta she had chosen to go on a low-dose pill. The dose must have been too low if this was the result.

Her heart lurched with a terrifying mixture of feelings.

Her first reaction after the initial shock had dimmed had been utter delight that Jacob's baby was growing deep inside her. Two hands crept down to smooth over her belly, imagining what he or she would look like. Tall and fair like Jacob, with sapphire-blue eyes, or dark-eyed with olive skin and curls like her own? If she could only be sure that it was either, and not like poor Matthew. . .'

'No! I couldn't bear it if it happened all over again.' She wrapped her arms tightly around herself and rocked backwards and forwards.

The phone rang again, jerking her out of her thoughts. She sat still on the settee as though spellbound until the machine answered the call.

'Louise. . .?' She heard him mutter something under his breath, then he spoke into the phone again. 'Call me when you get home, please. . .' Again, there was a long pause before he put the phone down, and Louise almost put her hand out to pick up the call but at the last minute she drew her hand back.

What could she say to him? He would want to know why she had come home; what was wrong. How could she tell him what the tests had revealed in a phone call?

How was she going to tell him when he came home? Her mind was racing round in circles trying to find a solution to the impossible situation.

If only. . . If only she and Jacob had never decided to change their agreement, then this situation would never have arisen. But then she would never have known how wonderful Jacob was as a lover. . .

Perhaps. . . Perhaps she could keep it a secret until she had a chance to arrange for an abortion?

Don't be stupid, she castigated herself. In the first place, Jacob is going to know as soon as he gets the results of those tests, and in the second place, you know damned well that you could never bear to kill his baby—especially as it may end up being the only part you have left of him when he discovers. . .

Oh, God, if there was only some way of finding out if this baby is like Matthew. She ran loving hands over her waist, marvelling at the tenacity of human nature. The very fact of the existence of this baby was a threat to everything and everyone she loved.

'Even though I've only known about your existence for a few hours,' she whispered aloud shakily, 'I love you already, just as I loved Matthew and I love Aletta now.'

The phone rang for the third time.

'*Om godswil*, Louise! Where are you? The car is still in the car park here and you're not answering the phone. *Ik begrijp het niet*.' She actually heard him draw in a deep breath then force it out between his teeth in a long hiss. 'Please, Louise. Ring the hospital. I. . .I need to speak with you. . . Please!'

When she heard him put the phone down, Louise found she was sobbing quietly to herself, tears running silently down her cheeks.

'Oh, Jacob, I'm sorry,' she wailed, remembering his halting words. 'None of this is your fault. It's mine. I never told you what could happen. . .

'Well, then——' she blew her nose loudly and scrubbed the tears from her cheeks '—if it's my fault, then it's up to me to do something about it.' She squared her shoulders and walked across the room towards the hall.

It must have been several hours later when she finally heard Jacob arrive home.

She had heard the phone ring several times but,

from the bedroom, she couldn't hear any messages being left.

His feet sounded in the hallway and she heard him opening each door in turn. Then, they were coming up the stairs two at a time.

She heard him pause outside Aletta's door; heard his brief mutter as he found her sleeping soundly and the soft sounds as he walked quietly across to her cot, knowing that he would be bending down to check her covers and stroke her soft cheek the way he always did.

Finally, he arrived at their bedroom door, pushing it wider so that the light from the hallway spread in a broad wedge across the carpet towards the bed.

He switched the light on and the glaring brightness made her close her eyes for a second.

'Louise!' He sounded shocked, but whether it was shock at seeing her surrounded by half-packed suit-cases or shock that she was there at all Louise couldn't tell.

He was silent for so long that she had to look at him, her eyes riveted by the stark pallor of his face and the dark emptiness of his eyes.

His hair was uncharacteristically dishevelled and his collar was undone, his silk tie pulled askew.

'Why were you sitting in the dark?' his voice sounded rusty, as if it hurt his throat to speak.

'I hadn't realised it *was* dark,' she whispered weakly, her pulse beating frantically in the base of her throat.

She put her hand up to cover the evidence of her agitation and discovered that she was holding the little frame containing Matthew's photo.

She had believed that there were no more tears left in her but as she gazed down on his perfect little face, two more crawled their way over her cheeks to fall onto her hands.

'Ah, Louise.' The sight of those tears had him walking towards her slowly, as if he was approaching an injured animal. 'I'm sorry you are so unhappy.' He stopped in front of her and sat himself down on the corner of the linen chest.

'You know?' Her eyes were dark with anguish as they met his and she saw him nod briefly.

'Why did you say you're sorry, then? It was what you wanted, wasn't it? I told you I couldn't give you a baby. I told you.' Her voice started to rise. 'It's just a mistake. I don't want to be pregnant. I can't. . .I can't have the baby. I'll lose everything. . .'

'*Nee*!' He shouted furiously, shaking his head. 'No. Not again! You will not try to kill my baby.'

'You don't understand,' she cried piteously. 'I daren't have it. . .'

'You will have no choice,' he thundered. 'I will have you arrested. I will fight you in your law courts if I have to but I will not let you kill my baby.'

'I don't want to kill it. . .'

'I didn't go to all that trouble. . .'

They spoke together and stopped simultaneously too, as each became aware of what the other was saying.

'You don't want to kill my baby? Then, what. . . Why did you. . .?' He gestured at the half-packed suitcases, wanting her to explain, but she was speechless for long seconds while she replayed what he had let slip.

'What did you mean?' Suddenly her voice was deathly calm and its very deliberate control caught his attention immediately.

'What? When?' He was genuinely puzzled.

'You said—"I didn't go to all that trouble. . .". What trouble? What have you done?'

Her eyes were riveted on his face so that she saw the tide of guilty colour sweep upwards.

'My God!' The words were filled with utter disbelief. She leapt up from the corner of the bed and whirled into the bathroom to wrench open the mirrored cabinet door. She rummaged frantically through the contents, sending most of them clattering down on to the vanity unit in her vain search.

'Where are they,' she shrieked. 'You liar! You cheat! Where are they?' She felt him arrive at the door, rather than saw him, and turned on him, her wild rage close to madness. 'What have you been giving me each night?' she demanded, then gave him no chance to answer.

'God! What a fool I've been!' she threw her hands up in the air and stormed backwards and forwards in a vain attempt to vent some of her anger. 'You would have thought I would have learnt my lesson with Colin but, oh, no. Here I go again, blindly trusting another liar.

'Well?' she finally halted in front of him, both hands clenched tightly into fists. 'What have you been feeding me? Sugar pills?' She flung her head back in challenge and glared up at him, completely undaunted by the fact that he was a foot taller and probably nearly twice her weight.

'Folic acid.' His deep baritone was utterly collected.

'I see.' Suddenly she was icily calm, her anger now under her control. 'So that made it all right, did it?'

'I knew you were afraid to have another baby, in spite of the fact you knew about the spina bifida research results. So——' his tone was so cool, so rational '——when I found out that you really wanted to have my baby, I. . .'

'How?' She fired the word at him with the speed of

a bullet. 'How could you be so sure that I wanted to have a baby?'

He was silent for a long time then, just as he drew breath to speak, she knew.

'My diary,' she whispered incredulously. 'You read my diary!' She staggered back several steps coming up against the side of the bath and sinking gratefully on to the side. Her knees were shaking so much she wasn't sure they would have supported her much longer.

'How dare you?' she breathed. 'Have you no sense of honour?'

'How else could I find out what you were thinking?' She must have touched a painful spot because suddenly his own anger ignited in a rare display. 'You said that even if we didn't have love in this marriage we would have honesty. Well, I ask you. How honest have you been?' His eyes were like twin lasers pinning her in place, cutting her to the bone.

'You have written that you want a baby. You have even written that you love me, but you have never said the words in plain English to my face.' He hadn't moved from his place in the doorway but his powerful presence filled the room. He was trying to dominate her just by the force of his will and Louise refused to allow it to happen.

'What about you?' she counter-attacked sharply. 'Is it honest to expect to make your wife pregnant whether she wants it or not, without even a discussion about it?' Her dark sherry eyes blazed up at him. 'In case it has slipped your notice, this is *my* body and it is my *right* to have a say in whether I conceive a baby or not.' Her words carried the force of utter conviction. 'How many times have I told you that I couldn't take the risk?'

'I too have spoken to you again and again. I have

tried to tell you that the chances of having another
baby like Matthew are negligible, but you would not
listen. Finally I knew that the only way was to prove
it to you.'

'Your arrogance is unbelievable——'

'Louise,' he broke into her tirade. 'You are a
wonderful mother to my Aletta and when I saw your
words in your diary—that you would love to have my
baby but you were afraid—then I knew it was only
your fear of losing another baby, the way you lost
Matthew, which was holding you back.'

'No,' Louise knew now that only the truth would be
enough to convince Jacob. Once again she would have
to tell her husband of the dark secret in her life. Last
time it had left her a widow with a dying son. This
time she risked losing her daughter and the man she
loved most in all the world.

'No,' she repeated. 'It was the fear of losing you.'

'Why? Why should you be afraid of losing me? I am
your husband. . .'

'So was Colin.'

'I am not the same as he was!' He was affronted by
the comparison.

'But you would feel the same as he did,' Louise
insisted. 'Especially with your colouring.'

'What?' Jacob ran his fingers through the silvery
thickness of his hair, the overhead lights gleaming on
each strand. 'What on earth does my colouring have
to do with anything?'

'You remember what Matthew looked like, of
course.' She straightened up from her position on the
side of the bath and walked towards him. Jacob
stepped aside to allow her to pass through to the
bedroom.

Walking over to her side of the bed, she bent to

retrieve the photo frame which had slid to the floor with her precipitate departure.

She handed the picture to Jacob.

'He doesn't look much like me, does he?' she challenged.

'Not his hair colour, but his features had quite a marked similarity. So what? There is no rule that says babies have to take after their mother.'

'You never saw Colin, did you?' She sounded utterly certain as she held out her hand for the frame.

She turned it over in her hand and twisted the little lugs which held the back in position and slid a second photo out from behind the first.

'That was Colin.' Her tone was flat as she handed him the small colour print. Colin smiled out at the world, his light brown wavy hair expertly cut, his pale blue eyes full of self-confidence.

She positioned the photo of Matthew in Jacob's palm so that it lay beside his father's.

'The first and only time Colin saw his son he called me a whore and denied paternity. If he had lived long enough he would have divorced me. Instead he killed your wife and nearly killed your daughter.' She laughed bitterly.

'He accused me of sleeping with other men, of breaking my marriage vows, when he was consistently unfaithful.' She waved a dismissive hand before she removed the final photo from its hiding place. 'That doesn't matter any more. It's in the past and it can't touch me any more. This——' she gazed down for a long moment before she looked up at him. 'This is a part of the past which has cast a shadow over my whole life.' And she handed it to him.

The photograph showed a couple standing with their arms around each other. The woman was an older version of Louise, her hair the same honey amber halo of curls but her eyes a limpid blue in a peaches-and-cream complexion. The man standing next to her was gazing straight at the camera, his eyes fiercely dark in the hawklike features of a startlingly handsome Native American man.

'They are my parents,' she declared bluntly. 'My mother and my father.' Her chin was tilted up as if in expectation of a blow.

'But. . .' Jacob hesitated. 'When we married you said you never knew your father.'

'My grandparents told me he died before I was born and that my mother left me with them to bring up. It wasn't until I contacted her when I got married to Colin that I found out the truth.

'My father was training as a doctor and had come over to England on some sort of exchange scheme for six months. He met my mother and they fell in love. At first my grandparents were quite happy for her to meet this young American doctor at the house of their own doctor. What better catch could there be for the apple of their eye than a soon-to-be-wealthy doctor!

'Then they met him and found out he was "coloured" and forbade my mother to see him again. That was when they discovered that I was on the way.

'Mother was under twenty-one and they refused her permission to marry, and they alerted the immigration authorities that my father had overstayed his visa. Finally, they came to an agreement. Mother would have me and hand me over to them to raise and then they would wash their hands of her.' Her voice was resentful.

'Did your mother never try to get you back?'

'I don't know. My grandparents refuse to speak of her. Whenever I tried to ask about my parents when

I was younger, I was given the impression that something bad had happened.'

'Were you afraid that this baby would look like its grandfather?' He indicated the photo.

'No. I would be proud for him or her to look like him. When I finally had a letter from my mother she told me about the work he does.' She smiled wryly. 'He became a paediatrician.'

Jacob gave a brief bark of laughter at the irony of coincidence before sobering again.

'If it wasn't that, then why were you so afraid?'

'I was afraid you would reject the baby, as Colin did.'

His laughter this time had a bitter ring to it.

'My God. If ever two people have been stumbling round each other in the fog.' He shook his head. 'If you did but know it, I would have been equally willing to suspect it came from *my* side of the family.'

'Yours!' She looked askance at the extreme blondness of his hair and the sapphire blue of his eyes. 'Why?'

He looked down once again at the photographs he held in his hand before squaring his shoulders and looking her straight in the eye.

'Because I have no knowledge at all of my parents.'

'They're both dead?' Louise's sympathetic heart was touched.

'I have no idea,' he said simply. 'I was a. . . .a foundling, I think you call it. Apparently someone was turning some rubbish over in a dustbin to try to find some food and found me in an old bag wrapped in a pillowcase. The two old men who handed me in to the police were called Jacobus and Rutger and the place they found me was. . .'

'Den Haag.' Louise finished.

'Exactly. From then on I was shunted from one home

to another until I became thoroughly institutionalised.'

'No wonder the idea of family is so vital to you, even more so than to me,' she exclaimed. 'Mine was far from ideal, but at least it exists.'

'In the end we made our own family. The children in the orphanage who remained in one place long enough to form bonds.'

Louise thought for a minute then smiled. 'Zuster Beckers!' she exclaimed.

'And Corrie, and others you'll meet when we go back again. They are my family in a way, but I hadn't realised just how important it was to me until the life of my child was threatened.

'Louise.' He paused to take the empty frame out of her hands and put it aside with the photos. He took both her hands in his and pulled her towards him. 'Louise, this baby you carry could be bright green all over for all I care. It is only important that he's ours and we love him and each other. I made sure that you were taking the recommended amount of folic acid so that I could tell you all your fears were over, but——'

'Do you?' she interrupted.

'Do I what?' She had stopped him in his tracks.

'Love me?' she clarified bravely, needing to know where she stood. 'You accused me of writing it but never saying it. Well, you've never said it either.'

'*Ik houd van jou*,' he said with utter simplicity.

'But you told me that means. . .'

'It means "I love you". . .' His eyes met hers candidly.

'But the first time you said that was. . .'

'The first time we made love. Yes. Then, when you asked me to teach you how to say it, I couldn't resist. I wanted to hear you say you loved me even if it was only by trickery.'

'That was so many weeks ago. Do you mean to tell me that you've loved me all that time?'

He took her in his arms and cradled her against the powerful length of his body. She tilted her head back to lean on the muscular breadth of his chest while she watched the expressions changing on his face.

'I think,' he said slowly, 'that I started to fall in love with you when I saw you caring for your baby. You were so sweet and gentle and loving.' His head came down until their lips touched, smoothly stroking from side to side in a gentle friction which made her eager for more.

His words were circling around in her head slowly being submerged in a rising tide of desire. Suddenly something floated to the surface and she jabbed a finger in his ribs.

'Oof!' he complained. 'What was that for?'

'What did you mean, "he"?' she demanded.

'I'm sorry.' He shook his head. 'I've lost you.'

'You called the baby "he". Does that mean you only want it if it's a boy?'

'Certainly not! I would love a little daughter with her mother's big sherry-brown eyes and toffee-coloured curls. Anyway,' he added glibly, 'if it's not a boy this time, we can always try again!'

He cradled her chin in one broad palm and raised it at the same time as he angled his own head to bring their mouths together in perfect alignment.

At the last moment Louise's fingers came up to cover his lips and prevent their contact with hers.

'Ah. I see.' Her eyes gleamed up at him. 'Were you keeping that little plan a secret?'

'No, *mijn lieveling*. No more dark secrets. Love has banished them all.'

\*     \*     \*

The tall man stood quietly in the shadows, watching. From the glassed-in area of Sister Harris's office, the whole of the ward was visible, but his gaze was fixed on one group of occupants.

The light above her bed outlined Louise's hair like a halo as she leant back against the banked pillows.

Her parents had just left after a very successful visit, taking Aletta home with them to Jacob and Louise's house where they were spending the next week.

The last six months had been a testing time with the gradual formation of bonds between them. They would probably never be close—they had spent too many years apart for that. But Jacob had hopes that it was the start of a friendship which would bind them all together with an affinity stronger than a mere blood tie.

As if she felt his gaze on her, Louise glanced up, unerringly looking straight towards the shadowy corner. She smiled in his direction, then back down at the treasure she held in her arms.

'Do you need any help?' The deep voice caressed her as he perched one hip on the edge of the bed.

'Your timing is impeccable, *mijn grote man*.' She laughed up at him as he tried to lean over the baby to steal a kiss. 'One baby ready for winding.' And she held her elbow out so that he could slide his hands underneath to lift a well-wrapped bundle on to his broad shoulder, the tiny head of blond curls seeming even smaller by comparison with his father's great size.

'How are you feeling now, my love?'

'Considerably lighter, thank goodness. That last month felt like a year, carrying these two.' She turned the second bundle against her own shoulder, the straight dark hair an uncanny echo of another baby and another time.

Jacob smiled broadly. 'I can't wait until these two

are old enough to start announcing that they're twins.'

Louise laughed with him and turned little Bernard round to face his father and younger brother. 'He got straight dark hair from my side of the family and sapphire eyes from yours, while Conrad inherited my father's dark eyes and your hair colour.'

'And your curls.' Jacob smiled, reaching out his free hand to stroke it over her hair.

'There is one thing I found a little worrying, though,' Louise mused.

'Something about the children?'

'Indirectly,' she confirmed, the sparkle in her eyes warning Jacob to brace himself. 'I noticed a definite pattern and I wondered if there's any significance in it? We now have three children, Aletta, Bernard and Conrad. That's A, B and C. Does this mean you've got a secret plan to fill a whole alphabet!'

'No, *lieveling*, I told you. No more secrets. I'm quite prepared to talk openly about the next twenty-three letters. After all, if you can manage them in multiples, it won't take long at all!'

He was still laughing as he leant towards her for his kiss, dodging her playful thump.

'Ah. . .' he surfaced long moments later. *Ik houd van jou, vrouw van me,*' he pledged solemnly.

'Then that's all that matters, my love.' And she smiled up at him, her eyes free of shadows at last.

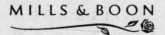

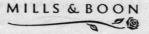

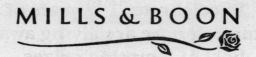

# MILLS & BOON

# LOVE  CALL

### *The books for enjoyment this month are:*

**ANYONE CAN DREAM**                Caroline Anderson
**SECRETS TO KEEP**                      Josie Metcalfe
**UNRULY HEART**                       Meredith Webber
**CASUALTY OF PASSION**               Sharon Wirdnam

---

### *Treats in store!*

Watch next month for the following absorbing stories:

**SMOOTH OPERATOR**                   Christine Adams
**RIVALS FOR A SURGEON**              Drusilla Douglas
**A DAUNTING DIVERSION**                Abigail Gordon
**AN INDISPENSABLE WOMAN**              Margaret Holt

---

Available from W.H. Smith, John Menzies, Volume One, Forbuoys,
Martins, Tesco, Asda, Safeway and other paperback stockists.

Readers in South Africa - write to:
IBS, Private Bag X3010, Randburg 2125.

# To celebrate 10 years of Temptation we are giving away a host of tempting prizes...

**10 prizes of FREE Temptation Books for a whole year**

— plus —

**10 runner up prizes of Thorntons delicious Temptations Chocolates**

**Enter our Temptation Wordsearch Quiz Today and Win!**

**10th** All you have to do is complete the wordsearch puzzle below and send it to us by 31 May 1995.

The first 10 correct entries drawn from the bag will each win 12 month's free supply of exciting Temptation books (4 books every month with a total annual value of around £100).

The second 10 correct entries drawn will each win a 200g box of Thorntons Temptations chocolates.

| I | F | G | N | I | T | I | C | X | E |
|---|---|---|---|---|---|---|---|---|---|
| A | O | X | O | C | A | I | N | S | S |
| N | O | I | T | A | T | P | M | E | T |
| N | B | V | E | N | R | Y | N | X | E |
| I | R | O | A | M | A | S | N | Y | R |
| V | C | M | T | I | U | N | N | F | U |
| E | O | H | U | O | T | M | V | E | T |
| R | N | X | U | R | E | Y | S | I | N |
| S | L | S | M | A | N | F | L | Y | E |
| A | T | O | N | U | T | R | X | L | V |
| R | U | O | M | U | H | I | A | A | D |
| Y | W | D | Y | O | F | I | M | K | A |

TEMPTATION
SEXY
FUN
EXCITING
TENTH

ROMANTIC
SENSUOUS
ADVENTURE
HUMOUR
ANNIVERSARY

**PLEASE TURN OVER FOR ENTRY DETAILS**

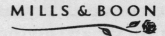

## MILLS & BOON

# HOW TO ENTER

**10** All the words listed overleaf below the wordsearch puzzle, are hidden in the grid. You can find them by reading the letters forward, backwards, up and down, or diagonally. When you find a word, circle it or put a line through it.

Don't forget to fill in your name and address in the space below then put this page in an envelope and post it today (you don't need a stamp). Closing date 31st May 1995.

Temptation Wordsearch,
**FREEPOST,**
P.O. Box 344,
Croydon,
Surrey
CR9 9EL

COMP395

Are you a Reader Service Subscriber?   Yes ☐   No ☐

Ms/Mrs/Miss/Mr _____

Address _____

_____

_____ Postcode _____